PRAISE FOR M. L. BUCHMAN

3x Top 10 Romance of the Year

— ALA BOOKLIST

Tom Clancy fans open to a strong female lead will clamor for more.

— DRONE, PUBLISHERS WEEKLY

(Miranda Chase is) one of the most compelling, addicting, fascinating characters in any genre since the Monk television series.

— DRONE, ERNEST DEMPSEY

(*Drone* is) the best military thriller I've read in a very long time. Love the female characters.

— SHELDON MCARTHUR, FOUNDER OF THE MYSTERY BOOKSTORE, LA

Superb!

— DRONE, BOOKLIST, STARRED REVIEW

M L. Buchman's ability to keep the reader right in the middle of the action is amazing.

— LONG AND SHORT REVIEWS

The only thing you'll ask yourself is, "When does the next one come out?"

— WAIT UNTIL MIDNIGHT,
ROMANTIC TIMES BOOK REVIEWS, 4
STARS

I knew the books would be good, but I didn't realize how good.

— NIGHT STALKERS SERIES, KIRKUS
REVIEWS

THE COMPLETE FIRE LOOKOUTS

A WILDFIRE ROMANCE SHORT STORY COLLECTION

M. L. BUCHMAN

Buchman Bookworks

Copyright 2020 Matthew Lieber Buchman

All stories previously published separately and in other collections. All introductory material is new.

Published by Buchman Bookworks, Inc.

All rights reserved.

This book, or parts thereof, may not be reproduced in any form without permission from the author.

More by this author at: www.mlbuchman.com

Cover images:

Young Man Home © Curaphotography | Dreamstime

Watch tower on Sunset Sky © Pklimenko | Dreamstime

SIGN UP FOR M. L. BUCHMAN'S
NEWSLETTER TODAY

and receive:
Release News
Free Short Stories
*a **Free** book*

Do it today. Do it now.
http://free-book.mlbuchman.com

CONTENTS

Other works by M. L. Buchman: *(* - also in audio)*

Thrillers

Dead Chef
Swap Out!
One Chef!
Two Chef!

Miranda Chase
*Drone**
*Thunderbolt**
*Condor**

Romantic Suspense

Delta Force
*Target Engaged**
*Heart Strike**
*Wild Justice**
*Midnight Trust**

Firehawks
MAIN FLIGHT
Pure Heat
Full Blaze
*Hot Point**
*Flash of Fire**
Wild Fire

SMOKEJUMPERS
*Wildfire at Dawn**
*Wildfire at Larch Creek**
*Wildfire on the Skagit**

The Night Stalkers
MAIN FLIGHT
The Night Is Mine
I Own the Dawn
Wait Until Dark
Take Over at Midnight
Light Up the Night
Bring On the Dusk
By Break of Day

AND THE NAVY
Christmas at Steel Beach
Christmas at Peleliu Cove
WHITE HOUSE HOLIDAY
*Daniel's Christmas**
*Frank's Independence Day**
*Peter's Christmas**
*Zachary's Christmas**
*Roy's Independence Day**
*Damien's Christmas**
5E
Target of the Heart
Target Lock on Love
Target of Mine
Target of One's Own

Shadow Force: Psi
*At the Slightest Sound**
*At the Quietest Word**

White House Protection Force
*Off the Leash**
*On Your Mark**
*In the Weeds**

Contemporary Romance

Eagle Cove
Return to Eagle Cove
Recipe for Eagle Cove
Longing for Eagle Cove
Keepsake for Eagle Cove

Henderson's Ranch
*Nathan's Big Sky**
*Big Sky, Loyal Heart**
*Big Sky Dog Whisperer**

Love Abroad
Heart of the Cotswolds: England
Path of Love: Cinque Terre, Italy

Other works by M. L. Buchman:

Contemporary Romance (cont)

Where Dreams
Where Dreams are Born
Where Dreams Reside
Where Dreams Are of Christmas
Where Dreams Unfold
Where Dreams Are Written

Science Fiction / Fantasy

Deities Anonymous
Cookbook from Hell: Reheated
Saviors 101

Single Titles
The Nara Reaction
Monk's Maze
the Me and Elsie Chronicles

Non-Fiction

Strategies for Success
Managing Your Inner Artist/Writer
*Estate Planning for Authors**
Character Voice
*Narrate and Record Your Own Audiobook**

Short Story Series by M. L. Buchman:

Romantic Suspense

Delta Force
Delta Force

Firehawks
The Firehawks Lookouts
The Firehawks Hotshots
The Firebirds

The Night Stalkers
The Night Stalkers
The Night Stalkers 5E
The Night Stalkers CSAR
The Night Stalkers Wedding Stories

US Coast Guard
US Coast Guard

White House Protection Force
White House Protection Force

Contemporary Romance

Eagle Cove
Eagle Cove

Henderson's Ranch
*Henderson's Ranch**

Where Dreams
Where Dreams

Thrillers

Dead Chef
Dead Chef

Science Fiction / Fantasy

Deities Anonymous
Deities Anonymous

Other
The Future Night Stalkers
Single Titles

INTRODUCTION

I blame this series entirely on Emily Beale—the heroine of my first Night Stalkers romantic suspense, *The Night Is Mine.* Not just the Fire Lookouts, but all five of the Firehawks series:

- The Firehawks (five novels)
- The Firehawks Smokejumpers (three novels)
- The Hotshots (five short stories)
- The Fire Lookouts (five short stories)
- The Oregon Firebirds (five short stories)

And that's assuming that I'm done with this series. I think I am, but I've been fooled before. I "knew" that I was done long before the Oregon Firebirds took their first flight.

Seriously. All Emily's fault. She did her job in the Night Stalkers series, which was to find four kick-ass soldiers to fill the four seats of her helicopter. The series was founded on filling the four seats of a Black Hawk helicopter with four strong women and the men they deserved. For myself, I call these the Emily Beale Quartet: *The Night is Mine, I Own the Dawn, Wait Until Dark,* and *Take Over at Midnight.*

The problem was that when Emily exited the Night Stalkers, I was far from done with her (or, closer to the truth, she was far from done with me). I think that she is one of the best characters I've ever created. So what would she do next?

She left the Night Stalkers because of her first pregnancy. No longer willing to fly at the tip of the military spear, she chose a safer career. I thought she'd fly as a trainer or become a commanding officer back at the field office, but that just wasn't her style.

Instead, she chose to start a whole new spin-off series.

Who knew?

Apparently she did, and the Firehawks series was born. The pilots who fly to fight wildland forest fires took off and Emily along with them.

Suddenly I was researching a whole new world: wildfires.

There were a hundred corners of fascinating jobs and duties to wander into.

LOOKING FOR THE FIRE

__Tess Weaver__ only feels at home on the top of the mountain above a thousand square miles of Idaho-Montana wilderness, watching for wildfires. It's the quiet place she makes sense to herself, alone in the sky.

Right until __Jack Parker__ becomes her closest neighbor, on the next ridge, one lookout tower and fifteen long miles away.

A magic summer, connected only by the wildfire watch and radio, they discover that they're both Looking for the Fire.

The Firehawks may have been born of Emily Beale. But the Fire Lookouts series was born out of a discussion with my wife.

Long ago, she wanted to work on a fire lookout tower. She went through all of the training at the top of her class. She scraped together the necessary gear from her meager savings. And then the head ranger refused to place a single woman out at a tower because of the risk to life and limb—despite the direct advice from trainers and other rangers.

Had the Internet existed at the time, she might have been able to find that Hallie Daggett was the first woman to serve as a lookout in 1913 and served for fifteen summers. Or pointed out that Nancy Hood was already a couple decades into her fifty-eight year career as a fire lookout. Not that either truth would probably have affected the anti-female bias that was so prevalent in the Forest Service. (Nancy had wanted to fight the fires directly, but had been forbidden to do so. The first female smokejumper had to fight her way onto a crew, almost literally, finally breaking that barrier in 1981.)

From the moment my wife told me her story, I knew I had to write the story that let her complete that journey. She is nothing like Tess Weaver, except for being a single woman headed to a fire lookout tower, but the story belongs to my wife.

I began reading blogs and books about the experiences of fire lookouts. Unlike with my Hotshots, I realized early on that I had a series here.

There's a strange community that exists among the lookouts. High atop the peaks, they are connected by radio and a vigilance for fire. They may never meet, but they are no less of a community for that.

So, I placed them deep in the Idaho wilderness and set them to watch for the fire.

1

---

ess Weaver had been waiting for this moment for months. Like a racehorse out of the gate she'd counted down; seasons, weeks, days, hours…

She hadn't slept a wink last night, caught in some half-waking nightmare that the freedom that beckoned from so close by would be torn away.

But the morning shone bright with that crystalline blue that could only exist above the Lolo National Forest which thrived along the Idaho-Montana border. The snows had released their stranglehold on the Selway-Bitterroot wilderness and the trails were finally open to her favorite season of the year, fire season.

Always sounded crazy that way, but since it was only inside her head, it didn't really matter. Did it?

Tess left behind the main roads, then the paved ones. Soon she was winding her little pickup along a narrow forest road. The only tracks were the team that had come up to inspect for washouts and clear downed trees. Now it was just her.

She was done with the seven grinding months of

working Missoula bars. Six beers, four shooters. Another round of eight Jell-O shots and a pitcher of something dark—that table wouldn't know the difference anymore if she shit in the pitcher rather than filling it with the most expensive stout on tap. (Sometimes her sense of humor was the only thing that survived those nights.) Five orders of, *Hell no, I'm not going home with you.* Two scotch rocks neat. *And if you call me "Hey, Blondie!" once more you'll be wearing this pitcher rather than drinking it.* Three more pints of lager, one of pale ale, and a whiskey sour. Two more servings of *Hell no…*

Her looks earned the attention, and more importantly the big tips, but that didn't mean she was going to choose herself a man that even thought of coming near a place like that.

No idea where else she was going to find "him," but it wasn't at the Spotted Pony Bar.

For seven months she'd done her servitude in the kick-ass cowboy bar in Missoula filled with broke college students and rich skiers come to conquer Montana Snowbowl by skiing all thirty-nine trails without dying in the process. Half of the runs were "Black Diamond"— most difficult—trails; that should kill at least of some of these dweebs, shouldn't it? Few made it more than a dozen runs before getting trapped in the swirl of this bar and a dozen more just like it that lined the road from the mountain into town—a strip locals avoided like the plague around two a.m. last call. Even the cops were careful driving this stretch after midnight.

Tess was finally done with bowing to the holy paycheck and getting home at three a.m. after clearing out and cleaning up the place before she could finally take off her mandatory cowgirl hat—at least the damn thing didn't have to be pink though a lot of the waitresses went that way at the Spotted Pony. The last time an Appaloosa had been near the place was probably during the 1877 retreat of the Nez Perce peoples; it was just that authentic.

Tess parked Snow Cone, her battered white Toyota pickup truck that no longer had a third gear, but thankfully second and fourth were still going strong, at the very end of the fireroad and took a breath.

Then another.

The city did that to her, even a small city like Missoula.

Made her cynical when she least expected it.

She was always torn that way. The social whirl could be fun and it was nice to be able to get a decent burger or a slice of pizza when you wanted to. Catching an action flick on the big screen had its points as well.

But it was the shorter half of the year that she lived for.

For the next five months she'd be queen of one of the most least accessible fire lookout towers anywhere in the Idaho wilderness. Far enough out that the only visitors were either crazy, or crazier.

She climbed out and leaned back against her truck, closing her eyes and just letting the thick forest air wash the city off her.

The merely crazy people who'd reach her tower atop Cougar Peak—eight miles from the nearest road and 8,859 feet into the sky—were very like her; out to walk, fish, and camp in one of the toughest and wildest forests left in the lower forty-eight states. The Bitterroots might top out around nine and ten thousand where the Beartooths to the east and the Lemhis to the west in

Idaho cracked twelve, but for expanse and ruggedness and sheer cussed toughness of country, she'd vote for the Bitterroots any day. So, the merely crazy folks might stop for a day if they reached her lookout.

The crazier people would whip through in an hour. They were the ones walking the CDT. The Continental Divide Trail was way high and seriously tough. The southbounders still had a month before the snow in Glacier Park backed off enough to begin their trek from Canada to Mexico.

The northbound walkers wouldn't reach her until later in the fire season because they'd begun back in March or April down where Mexico shared her border with New Mexico, a hundred miles into the harsh desert south of the Gila National Forest. By the time they'd spent six months afoot, they'd be racing the snows to the Canadian border. They blew through the Lolo so fast that she sometimes didn't even have a chance to come down from her lookout tower to greet them before they were gone again from her small meadow.

That meant, for five months, the vast quiet would be hers. She couldn't wait.

Two weeks up, three days down in town or off camping in the wild while a substitute came in. Repeat until the end of the fire season chased her back down, at times barely steps ahead of the first heavy snow. Over the last five seasons she'd ridden out plenty of early blizzards while still monitoring fires as they chewed through the valleys that spread thousands of feet below her. Only once had she been caught by a true snow and that had been seriously bad; a mistake she wouldn't make again.

Tess shouldered her pack and took a deep breath.

The tang of hot engine metal from the slow climb up the forest road that was little more than a dozer track. And…

There it was.

Nothing like it down in the valleys. High forest, bright with pine and sunshine but still thick with fern, berry, and sumac undergrowth. You could practically smell the wildlife watching her from the trees, assessing this new intruder.

Not new, she reassured them. *Same chick as last year and the one before. Back to watch the fire.*

The distinct "pik" call and hard rattle of a downy woodpecker somewhere back in the trees released the other birds and the woods came back to a symphony of life that had been momentarily frozen by the wheezing arrival of her truck.

Her pack weighed fifty pounds and would be grueling by the time she'd hiked the last five thousand feet and seven miles up to her lookout. She really shouldn't have bagged out on her winter workouts so often. She'd be hurting by the time she arrived.

Didn't matter, she was headed into the hills.

Another three hundred pounds of supplies remained heaped in the truck bed under a tarp. In a couple days a mule team, who made much of its spring income ferrying stock up to the lookouts, would come by and do the heavy lifting for her.

Tess patted her truck on the hood where it would sit and wait for ten days and turned toward the perfect solitude of the trees.

2

*J*ack Parker waved as Burt drove off. An arm raised casually out the window, a downshift to ease around the first curve, and his buddy was gone.

Jack stood by the trailhead. They'd unloaded a huge mound of supplies at the head of the road, which thankfully wasn't his task to buck up to the lookout. He pulled on his pack and faced the great unknown. Fir trees towered above him so tall they looked ready to topple down and kill him where he stood.

Stoopid!

Clarie and Mitch always made their summers up here sound so friggin' romantic. So, when Clarie found out she was pregnant and would be delivering right in the middle of the summer, he hadn't put up too much of a fuss about taking their place for a season. Not as if he had anything better to do.

He was used to living a little rough.

Retired Army, four years in the dustbowl. All of it living in CHUs with a couple hundred other grunts assigned to the Containerized Housing Units—which was just as luxurious as it sounded. Living rough wouldn't be an issue.

And landing in Montana due to lack of any other prospects was eating at his ego and his body. Burt, his college roommate, had given him the couch space cheap. But after two months it had given him a permanent kink in the back and he still didn't know what to do with himself.

So, he was going to sit by himself, stare at empty wilderness for hours waiting for a puff of smoke, and get his head screwed back on straight.

Yeah, that made perfect sense. Not.

Clarie said the trailhead was easy to find. After fifteen minutes of floundering through blackberry thorns and checking his cell phone a half dozen more times for signal strength that it didn't have the first time, he finally stumbled on it. It *was* easy to find, once you found it. Standing a few feet apart, two knee-high boulders marked what might be the entry into Mirkwood—an evil forest grown even more dire since the hobbits voyage on the way to slay the fire-breathing dragon.

Fire.

He was headed to the top of a mountain to face a forest that breathed fire.

"Okay, Mirkwood. Here we go."

He resettled his pack with a grunt; he hadn't done a long hike with a full ruck since Basic. He'd been driving a MaxxPro MRAP for the last four years, and better yet, lived to tell about it. Wished he could have brought his fifteen-ton Mine Resistant Ambush Protected beast home. Blown up seven times and only lost two guys total out of a half jillion trips with ten troops typically onboard for each ride. An IED had blown out half their tires, then been followed up by a couple of T-men lying in wait for them to dismount. Two Army and two Taliban was the body count for that day—only deaths in the whole theater.

Still, it had gotten pretty shaky there toward the end. As the troops drew down, those remaining were blown up more often. Three of the IED strikes had been in his last three weeks in. And the T-man, with fewer targets, was shooting a lot more lead at his MRAP's armor hoping to find a hole. When he lay down to sleep at night, he could still here the deafening rattle of the gunfire pinging off his vehicle.

Not there anymore. Now here. He'd been saying that to himself a lot lately.

The pack. The trail. Hold the focus. Get your heavy-ass load moving.

Of course now, without the "Three A's" of ammo, armor, and more ammo—which still felt weird as hell, like he was walking around naked—the weight he carried wasn't all that different.

He'd grown up in downtown Phoenix. Going to college in Missoula hadn't exactly turned him into an outdoorsman, neither had driving an MRAP. Most of his time in the wilderness had been during Basic in the swamps and hills of South Carolina.

He inspected the forest as he began the long climb through it. Fir trees, maples, and ferns; those he knew. And blackberry thorns; his arms still itched from all the scratches. The white bark was either birch or aspen. After that, there were bushes and there were trees—his two primary classifications of stuff that grew outdoors.

Flowers didn't really count as they mostly grew in expensive florist shops and in girlfriend's vases, while they lasted. There'd been plenty of girls who hadn't lasted as long as the colored blooms.

What had he been thinking? Jack Parker. Wilderness.

Well, at least this trail was clearly marked. He checked his GPS, which suggested a shortcut that Claire had warned him against.

"Your machine doesn't know about the landslide that wiped out that trail three years ago. We had to cut in a new path that summer."

He stuck with the double-white trail blazes Mitch had sprayed on the trees every hundred yards or so.

3

ess kept her eyes on the trail, not looking at the view. Not yet. Saving that.

Cougar Peak tower was a two-story ten-by-ten foot building perched atop a broad pinnacle of rock.

The only approach was across a small meadow. Beyond that, she hiked the last hundred feet along the guide chain up the bare rock to the mountain's peak.

She entered the lower cabin first.

The cabin only had a normal winter's worth of bug corpses to sweep out; no mice or squirrel had gotten inside to nest this last winter, thank god. They could really mess a place up, leaving stinking patches where the mice peed in their own nests. That took a lot of bleach to clear away.

The water cistern was full to overflowing with rainwater and snowmelt off the tower roof. Best water in the world—tasted of cold sunshine. She dumped out the last of her city water, good riddance, and refilled her bottle from the cistern.

She could feel she was still moving at city pace as she

unloaded most of her pack into the rough shelves that were her cupboard. Whatever internal switch that eventually shifted to "move slower" hadn't yet been thrown.

With the cabin squared away and airing out through the open door and four small windows, Tess went back outside and climbed the exterior ladder. It led up to the narrow walkway that encircled the tower's upper story.

She circled the tiny deck that surrounded the tower on all sides, lifting clear the heavy shutters, feeling the sun's warmth radiating off their rough surface. They had protected the big, wrap-around glass windows through the brutal winter storms, but now, for five months, those windows were for her to see the world.

Duck inside—definitely needed to oil the lock—a quick floor sweep and it was all in order.

Out of the small pack she'd brought up from the cabin, she unloaded the last of it. Her radio, spare batteries, solar charger set to one side. Binoculars and the refilled water bottle to the other. Ammonia in a spray bottle and a squeegee. She took her time removing a season's worth of wind-borne mud and dust off the glass.

Then she stood in the center of the tower, the center of her world, and braced her hands on either side of the Osborne Fire Finder.

And let herself look up.

The world slapped her, just as it always did. In some directions she could only see a dozen miles before a ridge or peak blocked her view. In other directions a hundred miles of National Forest sprawled over knife-edge ridges and slashed canyons.

Ten miles to the east lay State Route 12, thankfully

invisible at the bottom of a valley. Past that, her view continued in an uninterrupted vista eighty miles to Flathead Lake and the Flathead National Forest beyond.

In all of the 360 degrees, even with her binoculars, the only human habitations she could actually see were two distant cabins and three even more distant lookout towers.

Once her survey was complete, by naked eye and binocular, she grabbed her radio and dialed in the Forest Service frequency.

"Dispatch. Over."

"Dispatch here. Go ahead. Over."

"Cougar Peak in service." You always reported by your location. Tess liked that. As if she herself embodied the mountain and she could leave her own name mostly behind for the rest of the summer.

"Roger that, Cougar Peak. Glad to have you back, Tess."

"Thanks, Vic. Glad to be here." Vic was the base commander for the whole area.

Tess kicked the single mattress on the narrow bunk, causing it to unroll. She usually slept in the tower, only her supplies below.

She collapsed on it face down. Though the official start of fire season was still over a week away, her internal alarm snapped her awake after only an hour's rest to scan the trees for a telltale puff of smoke that indicated a new fire.

"Uh, hello? Testing?"

Tess glared at the radio and wondered what idiot was on the freaking Forest Circus frequency. And more amusingly, just what Vic was going to do to them. This early in the season he was probably going to play nice.

"This is dispatch," Vic always gave someone the benefit of the doubt. That's why he was Dispatch and Tess was locked away in her steel gray-and-wood tower all summer. She wouldn't trade places for the world.

"This is Jack, uh, I mean Gray Wolf Summit."

"In service," Dispatch prompted.

"Yeah, right. In service."

"Roger that, welcome aboard, Jack."

Wait!

Gray Wolf Summit?

Not stopping to think, she grabbed up her radio, "Who the hell is this?"

Vic knew better than to answer.

"You. Gray Wolf. Who is this?"

"This is Gray Wolf Summit, go ahead."

"Where's Clarie and Mitch?"

"She's having a baby. I'm Gray Wolf for the summer."

Shit! Tess didn't like it. For the next five months her world was made up of the five closest lookout towers—two of which she couldn't see from here but had important overlapping sightlines for pinpointing a blaze. Beyond that there was only Dispatch and the occasional firefighting crew.

And all that was just the way she liked it.

Now, with no one asking her, no warning at all, this new guy. It was like coming home on college break only to find out that your best friend had moved away from next door to Texas or some such ridiculous place.

"Uh, welcome." She did her best not to sound too upset but expected that she didn't really pull it off.

"Is this Tess Weaver?" the radio voice asked. It sounded amused with itself.

"Cougar Peak to you." That didn't come out sounding as funny as she intended.

Laughter came back over the radio. A guy who laughed at her joke rather than assuming she was just plain nasty. Another chunk of city-born bitch shield slid off Tess and tumbled off the tower to shatter on the rocks below.

"Yeah, sorry. This is Tess. You're Jack…" she left it open as a question.

"That's Gray Wolf Summit to you. Over and out."

Well, if that didn't beat all. A guy with a decent sense of humor.

*J*ack left the radio on, though he had no intention of replying.

Not a sputter or a squawk came in.

Clarie had talked about how sweet Tess was; all alone in her tower summer after summer. Mitch's expression had been less forgiving about why she was alone. Princess in a tower or bitch on a rock? He was gonna side with Mitch on this one.

Jack had only one bar on his cell phone off some distant tower. Claire had told him there was reception, but this was sad. It flickered briefly up to two bars which he found ridiculously encouraging. It made him feel at least somewhat connected. He called Burt to say he'd arrived and wasn't—as his buddy was kind enough to predict at length over their final couple beers last night —ready for immediate evac.

Jack had stayed several beers later than he'd intended; he'd sure enjoyed watching the bartender. Long blondes were generally more trouble than they were worth, but this one had been something special.

Not just her figure—which had been decidedly athletic in those tight jeans and cowboy shirt untucked with the tails tied across her flat belly—or her shower of blond hair.

What had really caught him was the combination of an absolutely no-nonsense attitude, yet how easily she laughed and joked with the patrons. It didn't look like a sham, even if it had coaxed an extra ten-spot out of his pocket when Burt left the tip. Lady like that, who looked like that, wasn't gonna be interested in his down-and-out sorry self anyway. Especially not the night before he left for five months to serve a sentence in solitary.

His lookout tower was an all-in-one cabin in the sky. His toilet was a wooden outhouse fifty feet downslope from his tower. At the top of the tower's thirty-seven steps was a fourteen-foot square box surrounded by glass and topped by a radio antenna and a big-ass lightning rod.

Lightning, hadn't thought about that one.

Or the heavy guy wires that stretched out to every side, bolted into bedrock, to keep what must be titanic winds from wiping his temporary home over the cliff and into the valley that was freakily far below.

He'd had the mandatory couple days of classroom training, but the place was still a goddamn mystery. Mitch had planned to hike in with him to show him the ropes, then he'd sprained his ankle in a game of pick-up ball, so Jack was on his own.

The big two-foot disk of the Osborne Fire Finder stood on a pedestal in the middle of his tower cabin. It had a circular map of the area and a pair of sights mounted on a ring that spun around it.

He studied the map, which covered an enormous area and began picking out landmarks.

East and West Goat Mountains.

Sugarloaf Peak.

Como.

The Lonesome Bachelor.

Yeah, there was a good joke. Corporal Jack Parker (U.S. Army retired) who'd found a job staring at trees. Sure wasn't going to find anyone to cuddle with up here.

Clarie and Mitch were at the dead end of a long, tough trail that only connected to the lookout tower. Last year they'd had three visitors, total. One had been the mule train supplier who'd delivered their stock of goods.

Medicine Point Lookout.

Cougar Peak.

Tess Weaver. He spun the Osborne until it lined up perfectly on the map and then looked through the sights. Once he was sure he knew which peak it was, he grabbed for his binoculars.

His closest neighbor, fifteen miles away. Even the big glasses that Mitch had loaned him barely resolved the lookout tower as separate from the rocks.

Which was just fine.

Didn't need her anyway.

6

Jack was surprised at how quickly the days become routine. He rolled out with first light. Hauled up a gallon or two of water to get him through the day and made a quick breakfast of oatmeal and maple syrup with hot chocolate as the sunrise lit the horizon with a thousand shades of pinks and yellows.

After the sun broke the horizon, he'd go for a quick trail run. Didn't need to go more than five K to work up a good burn. No sweat, it evaporated in the high, thin air, but his muscles and the salt stains on his t-shirt told him he was working it hard on the steep and rugged grades.

Each morning held some surprise. A family of gray squirrels, a doe picking her way ever so delicately through the undergrowth, a bear who had surprised the shit out of him.

He'd rounded a sharp bend in the trail, circled around the next boulder, and almost run head on into the bear. His squawk, her furry roar of surprise, and they both instantly headed back the way they'd each come. He'd practically levitated back to the tower, not breaking from a dead sprint for almost a thousand feet of vertical gain. He'd sat and laughed at himself, wondering which of them had been more surprised, but only after he was in his tower and had the trapdoor closed and bolted from the inside.

Then there was the daily radio routine.

Nine a.m.

"Bare Cone Lookout in service. No smoke."

"Spot Mountain in service. No smoke."

"Cougar Peak in service. No smoke."

Then it was his turn.

He hadn't spoken directly to Cougar Peak since that first time, but he liked the sound of her voice. Efficient, clear, and well practiced.

Fifteen minutes later he'd stumble through his peak weather report: percent cloud cover, high and low temperatures, relative humidity, wind speed and direction, precipitation, and so on. He was always forgetting one item or another, even though it was listed right there on his log.

Tess Weaver was a machine, rattling it all off in half the time, almost in a single breath, in that totally female voice of hers that was teasing him across the airways. Probably one of those thin desiccated fifty-year olds.

Nine a.m. to six p.m. and they were done. Fires peaked between noon and four when the sun dried out the foliage and the midday heat led to stronger circulating winds. By six, the worst of the day was over.

Except so far there hadn't been anything at all.

Routine broke on the ninth day of his first tenner.

Nine days and there hadn't even been a cloud. He'd

run out of guys to text; they were either out of the Army long enough to have busy lives, or they were still soldiers and had even less to say to someone gone civvy.

He'd already read all five books he'd brought, twice. Definitely got to get more during his days off. Maybe some movies, but then he'd need another solar charger, a player, and a bunch of disks because wi-fi on top of the mountain peak, not so much.

"Dispatch, this is Cougar Peak. I have a smoke at three-sixteen point four degrees, approximately fourteen miles. Gray Wolf Summit, can you give me a cross? It might be behind a ridge for you."

Jack felt as if he'd just been electrocuted.

He looked down at the map. Three hundred and sixteen degrees from Cougar Peak. He rested his thumb on the mileage scale. About a thumb width and half for fourteen miles. That put it almost due west of him.

Grabbing his binoculars he hurried to the window. There was an awful lot of country out that way. The next road or town in that direction was Moscow, Idaho a hundred miles away—the great trackless waste of central Idaho.

"I don't see it," he sent after the first couple minutes of searching.

"Try looking closer to you," Cougar's voice came over the radio. She didn't follow that with, "Common beginner's mistake is looking too far away," which he appreciated.

It was…Holy Crap! The smoke was just one valley over. A thin pillar of white smoke wandering lazily into the air.

"I got it!"

"Okay," Tess teased him. "Take a breath, Big Bad Wolf, and shoot a cross sight so we can triangulate a fix."

He lined up the Osborne, "Two seven three degrees. Dead on."

"Roger that. I make it fourteen point three miles for the cross. Down in the guts of Loco Creek. Your fire."

Jack held his radio with both hands because he needed to hold something to keep his hands steady.

"What do you mean? You spotted it."

"It's in your territory."

His first fire and he got to name it. "How about Harold?"

The laugh that came back over the radio was musical and bright. It shocked the hell out of him. Who knew Cougar Peak could laugh like that. "The name is supposed to relate to the topography. And sorry, my end of Loco burned last year so I already used the obvious name."

"I knew a pretty crazy dude named Harold once." He had a tendency to not bother with body armor and Jack had seen him more than once walk through a hail of bullets unscathed as if he were untouchable. "How about Crazy Creek Fire? You sure that's not just someone's campfire?"

"There's been no lightning, so it actually was someone's campfire. There's only the one smoke, so it's probably not a pyromaniac. Except it's not a campfire anymore. When you can see that much smoke, it's already dug in and burning. Dispatch, we've got the Crazy Creek Fire, credit to Gray Wolf, I'd call it at an acre and growing fast. Just at the end of Forest Road 320-Alpha so watch for a camper or car racing to get off the mountain though they're probably long gone."

"Roger that. We'll get an engine out there to give it a look. Well done. Out."

Jack still felt giddy with adrenaline. He really needed to share it with someone. In the Army there'd always been the other guys in the MRAP that day or the CHU that night. He thought about calling Burt, but he wouldn't really understand.

Something had him picking up the radio.

"Hey, Cougar Peak?"

"Go ahead."

How did you boil such a feeling down into something that could be transmitted through a radio? A feeling as if he'd made a difference. Not just trucked teams back and forth across some section of hell as a living target in a massively armored vehicle, but might actually be saving some forest, even lives.

"Uh, thank you."

Her voice was soft when it came back over the radio, "You're welcome, Mr. Big Bad Gray Wolf. And welcome to the Freaking Forest Circus."

Ha! That was perfect. He was being paid to sit and be bored out of his skull. But in one instant, he'd jumped from useless to really helping. A circus act indeed.

"Roger that, She-lion."

She clicked her transmit button in acknowledgement but didn't speak again.

7

Tess wasn't sure how it had begun.

They'd talked at different times as the number of fires increased with the deepening season. When he spotted his first one on his own, she thought he was going to have kittens. It juiced him up something wild, reminding her of the joy in her first season—a feeling that hadn't diminished with time. It was that was grand to hear someone else who felt that way.

He settled well into working radio relay for the hand crews too deep in the canyons for their bosses to hear. Even on the Colgate Fire—which he'd named for being along Crest Creek—when there were six lines of madness going at once, he handled the radio fine. The airshow on that one had been impressive, huge air tankers lumbering by their towers just a few hundred yards straight out the windows. Helicopters painted black and fire-red whirling through the valleys and ridges. The airborne incident commander circling high above in his plane too busy to keep up with the ground relays. A fine piece of radio work, more than she'd have been able to handle on her first season.

So, the man had both a sense of humor and skills. Probably had a wife and kids down below that he only saw every other weekend. A couple times she came close to asking, but stopped herself. The Forest Service frequency was about business and—

"Hey, Cougar Peak. You there?"

"This is Cougar, go ahead Gray Wolf."

"Wanna dial up four tenths?"

"Sure." After six p.m., they were off the clock unless there was an active blaze close by.

They re-tuned their radios to a frequency off the Forest Service frequency by zero-point-four megahertz. And as the evening waned, they talked about nothing for half an hour before going to sleep with the sun.

On another night he asked, "You play chess?"

"Sure, but I don't have a board up here."

"Bring one after your next break."

And she did. They played radio chess through much of June and the fires of July.

Their three days off every two weeks never matched, so they were connected only eight work days out of every fourteen.

A couple times she almost hiked into Gray Wolf Summit on her days off, but she didn't want to ruin the illusion.

The time in July when her substitute couldn't make it because of car trouble, she gladly skipped the luxury of a city shower and a couple nights at her mom's place in order to stay in the sky and talk to Jack the Big Bad Gray Wolf.

"Tell me about you out in the world."

That stopped her.

"No. No, I don't think so."

"Big secrets?" he teased.

"It's not that." If not, what was it? "I don't want to think about those months. These months are the ones when I'm myself. This is where I belong." Which was true…and a total lame-ass evasion. *I don't want to spoil the illusion.*

She'd had plenty of relationships, with the usual good-bad ratio. Nothing that stuck. Nothing that felt as real as when she sat in the sky and looked down on the world made of forest.

"What do you look like, up there in your Cougar Tower? Give me something to go on."

"Sixty-five, round as a washtub, with bottle-red hair, and those stretchy pants in bright paisley green? You?"

"I's jes a bow-legged old cowhand, Ms. She-lion. Thas all I be."

"Your cowboy accent sucks." But still it made her laughter echo about the tower.

"What? Did I sound human there for a moment?"

"No, it wasn't that bad."

During the day, they were all business on the Forest Service frequency. But at night she sometimes fell asleep listening to him talk about his day, not that it was all that different from hers, but she liked to hear about it anyway. He didn't push again about the outside world as July rolled into August.

It was the crash that woke her with a shout of surprise. She'd slept down in the lower cabin that night, though she wasn't sure why.

A moment later, a blinding light filled the cabin brighter than daylight. An instant later, another flash. In the same instant, a deafening blast of superheated air as it was torn apart shook the walls hard.

There was no point counting seconds, the flash and boom of lightning and thunder were wrapped around each other like crazed lovers gone wild in the dark of the night. Instead she counted strikes, losing track around forty-seven. The tower and the peak were struck as if by a hailstorm of billion-volt hammers of Thor.

When it tapered off, she edged up to a window. The cool night air slipping over the windowsill reeked of ozone.

She'd ridden out some bad storms, though nothing like this. She remembered the terror of the first time a strike had hit her tower while she was in it. And that had been a single strike; this was a seriously wild.

It was rolling north, straight for Gray Wolf Summit. He didn't have a ground-level lower cabin like hers, his tower was his cabin. Jack was going to be right in the thick of it in a minute.

"Jack!" she shouted over her radio. "Jack! Wake the hell up!"

"Huh, what?"

"There's a lightning storm heading your way. Bad one! Do not try to leave your tower. The lightning rod and guy wires are your best protection. Lie on the wooden floor. Get off your bunk and don't touch anything metal. You got that?"

"Got it. I'm under the Osborne table and—" There was an unholy crash over the radio at the same moment she saw the strike from across the fifteen miles.

His scream was one of the most horrific sounds she'd ever heard.

Not surprise. Not fear. Stark terror.

She cried out his name, but there was no answer.

It would be impossible for him to hear under the storm of multiple strikes piling up on him.

No sound but that one scream and the crash of thunder. Fifteen seconds later, the muted roll that was only now starting to reach her through the fifteen miles of ozone-laden air that separated them.

Somewhere in the middle of it he transmitted a garbled message degraded into unintelligibility by the thunder on his end. It sounded like barely controlled panic. He might have shouted for her to keep talking. Actually, it hadn't sounded so controlled.

So she did. Shouting messages of comfort for fifteen seconds, listening for five. Shouting again.

Her voice grew hoarse, but she didn't stop.

Not even to wipe at the tears streaming down her cheeks.

8

---

*J*ack heard a voice somewhere. Far away. Calling him back.

Starting and stopping.

Calling to him until he came to.

He'd gone fetal on the floor of his lookout cabin. Cradled to his chest was a radio—it kept calling to him.

A woman.

Cougar Peak.

He managed to double-click the transmit key during her next break.

"Oh thank god! I thought you'd been incinerated or something." Her voice was thick, hoarse…as if she'd been shouting for a long time.

"How long?" his voice sounded even worse. The mere whisper hurt like hell.

"Storm moved out twenty minutes ago."

He swallowed and tasted blood. A little testing. Ow, shit! He'd bit his tongue really badly. Bit, hell. Felt like he'd ground it for the whole twenty minutes with his molars.

The bitter adrenal taste mixed with the iron of the blood almost made him sick. The only way he managed to resist it was knowing that if he puked all over the cabin floor, he was the one who'd have to clean it up. And god, she'd hear it.

Twenty minutes.

It had felt like twenty hours. He had been trapped in IEDs. Not one or two, but thousands: his MRAP tumbling across a field of them, each roll tossing more dead bodies, more deadly shards of steel, striking more IEDs which made him roll again, and more—

"Talk to me, Tess. It's bad. Just keep talking to me."

So she did. She told him about her first trip into the woods. Her mother taking her to see a lookout tower when she was just six.

"Mom wanted to be a lookout so badly. Did ground-school training and everything. Then the head ranger in charge of assignments said he wasn't going to let a single woman go out into the woods alone—couples and males only. She'd tried a dozen different regions, but they all said the same. It was that same summer she was raped in a city, because cities are so much safer than the deep woods, you know. That's how she had me. She never married."

"Is that why you're out here, She-lion?" He sat up. Every one of his muscles complained. He'd only had PTSD attacks a couple times. Figured it was going away. Yeah, until he rode through the heart of the lightning storm from hell.

"Maybe. First year it probably was. But we hiked in the woods a lot together. She liked, likes to fish. Has a bum knee now, so she can't get up here to see me, but we still walk into fishing spots. I fell in love with the wild on my own. Sometimes it feels like I can't breathe until I'm up here."

God but he could picture her, the goddess of the peaks. The she-lion standing guard over her wilderness.

"How about you?"

"Me?"

"You, Gray Wolf. Why are you out here?"

Why was he?

Truth?

"I couldn't think of anything better to do with my summer."

9

*T*ess took his phone number at the end of the season, she didn't have a number to give other than her mom's and Tess never gave that out.

"I'll buy the first beer," he'd offered.

She'd been down a week and still hadn't call to take him up on the offer.

Knew the number by heart, had it memorized before she'd lowered and latched the shutters, locked the site down for winter, and headed down the mountain.

Had almost dialed it from her mom's, but didn't know what to say. After the lightning storm, they'd gone deep. They'd told each other the important stuff, back and forth each night on their private frequency.

She felt as if her every truth had been exposed for him to see. Hollowed out trees, cracked wide to reveal their burned out hearts.

If she spoke to Jack Gray Wolf with no last name… if she met him, would she be able to still be herself? No one else knew what he now knew about her. She'd blow it for sure.

Harry took her back on at the Spotted Pony; bars were a pretty good fit for flaky seasonal work. Good bartenders were little better than itinerant workers, so there was always an opening.

Two lagers. Three tequilas with salt and lime. A pair of boilermakers. Two *Thanks but no thanks.* (That would turn into the *Hell no!* version somewhere in the next seven months as it always did.)

Two guys came and sat at the end of the bar.

She kind of remembered them from her last night before the fire season. Not that either had been that memorable. But they'd stayed late on her last night and tipped really well.

Her bartender's eye drifted over one of them, still unmemorable, but stopped on the other.

Was it really the same person? There was a set to the eyes, a depth and certainty that couldn't have been there before. Someone terribly alive lived in that face.

Harry served them, but she made a point of using the taps down that end of the bar for the next beers she had to draw.

The night was still quiet enough to overhear their conversation.

"You sure she even exists? Sounds like the horseshit craziest story you ever laid on me."

"She exists. She's real. Way more than you, asshole."

Tess was paralyzed with shock. The beer ran out of the glass over her fingers and began running along her forearm to dribble off her elbow. She startled and slapped the tap closed, wiped her hand and arm with a bar rag.

She'd know that voice anywhere. All summer it had been burned into the landscape of her thoughts until she knew it as well as her own. She knew the shape of every scar on his soul just as he knew the scars on hers.

Tess delivered the beer back down the bar.

Before she could talk herself out of it, she grabbed a pen and a bar napkin and wrote a quick note.

Drawing a fresh pint of the porter he was having, Tess set the napkin down with the message showing and then placed the beer right on top of it without saying a word. He'd know her voice as surely as she knew his.

Tess turned to the next patron calling for a refill even as he called out a confused, "Who's this from?"

From the corner of her eye, she saw him lift the beer and read the note.

Apply liberally in case of forest fire or lightning storm. She'd drawn a cougar's paw print for a signature.

He looked at her in absolute shock. She set down the beer she was pouring and turned to face him.

A hundred emotions ran across his features, ones that she found she could read as easily as her own; she might not know the handsome face, but she knew the man behind it so well that she didn't need to. There was no one she knew better, or who knew her better.

With a shout of pure joy, the same shout she heard in her heart each time she entered the wilderness, he vaulted the bar and rushed to stop a single step from her.

"She-lion?" his voice hesitated just as it did on that first fire call, right before he'd whispered that "Thank you" that had melted her heart.

"Hey there, Gray Wolf."

He reached for her, thought better of it, then brushed a finger as lightly down her cheek as the last breeze of a storm clearing off the horizon.

"You're real," he was as breathless as he'd been spotting his first fire.

"Last I checked."

This time when he went to reach for her, she stopped him with a hand against the center of his chest. The shock was as super-charged as a lightning strike and heated her insides to full burn.

"One question."

"Anything."

"What's your last name? Jack, Big Bad Gray Wolf, what?"

"Parker. Jack Parker."

She slid the hand up his chest, cupped his neck with her hand and pulled him down into a kiss. He didn't hesitate a second.

As she melted against him to the cheers of the bar crowd, she had just the least little glimpse of the future, like the first smoke puff that showed early to tell of the fire that would rage through the forest.

No longer the lone princess in her tower. Next year she'd be sharing lookout duties on Cougar Peak, and the year after, and the one after that, and...

FIRE AT GRAY WOLF
LOOKOUT

Life's deeper purpose eludes **Tom Cunningham,** *and its lesser purpose too. Leaving behind Seattle, his job, and a near endless supply of easy women, he grabs adventure and spends a summer in the Montana wilderness —looking for wildfires and also for himself.*

Done with her military service, **Patty Dale** *enters the wilderness to pursue her life's dream—to hunt gray wolves with a camera and a notebook.*

They both find far more than they bargained for when there's Fire at Gray Wolf Lookout.

For this story, several pieces came together. I write a lot of alpha heroes in my romantic suspense series (both male and female alphas). In *Fire at Gray Wolf Lookout* I wanted to write about two normal people with unusual occupations.

He is a fire tower lookout.

She is a wildlife biologist specializing in wolf behavior. The idea for this came from talking with an actual wolf biologist.

He was given a patrol area and a radio. He set camera traps and recorded all the behaviors and pack activities across a massive range of the Canadian wilderness. Once a week he would climb to the top of a high ridge so that he could radio in that he was alive. He would also send a summary report and note if he was desperate for some supplies that might be helicoptered in the next time there was a supply run.

Immediately after, in the next valley over, another wolf biologist radioed in her own report. After they were done, the two of them took to chatting over the radio.

When they were finally extracted close ahead of the coming winter, it was the first time they met. By then, their future was already set. They've since gotten their graduate degrees together, had children, and are continuing to pursue that which they love most, wolf and other mammal wildlife biology. (Seriously, you can't make this stuff up. Life is truly stranger than fiction.)

This character isn't either of them—Patty Dale is very much her own person—but her passion for the wolves is completely theirs.

1

$\mathcal{T}$he view of the Lolo National Forest on the Idaho-Montana border spread for a hundred miles in every direction. And Gray Wolf Summit fire lookout tower commanded one of the most beautiful and most remote regions of the forest. From his perch Tom Cunningham could see much of the Lolo, a big chunk of the Clearwater, and even the north tip of the Selway-Bitterroot Wilderness.

Despite being in his mid-twenties, he felt like the luckiest kid in the U.S. Forest Service. No one was watching, so what the heck, he spit off the edge of the tower. Like a twelve-year old, he watched it was the light breeze carried past the cliff and down into the canyon— he watched it as long as he could.

The whole acting-his-age thing had never really worked for him anyway, and someday he'd have to apologize to his parents for that. Both professors at the University of Washington—English lit Dad and Mom the chemist—and Tom had used his degree in geology to be an auto body shop mechanic.

His rut was obvious, didn't need to be on the outside to see it, Tom could feel it from the inside just fine. Like the crippled vehicles that streamed through his shop door, he couldn't seem to drive straight down any path…and that was on the rare occasions when he got running at all.

Screw that!

Last winter he'd gotten so sick of himself that he figured the best solution was to get away—way away!

He'd grown up in Seattle's Wallingford neighborhood, side-by-side housing that would be suburbia if it wasn't now tucked well inside city limits. It was also saved from that awful fate because the houses were fifty to a hundred years old rather than tract built pillboxes.

However, his experience with the great outdoors was limited to a couple of trips out to Snoqualmie Falls, a two hundred-and-fifty foot waterfall up in the Cascades. A good place for taking a girl on a nice date as the lodge had an excellent brunch.

His present situation, atop a Montana fire lookout tower, had been Lucy's idea. After six months of sharing a bed most nights she'd told him to go jump into a fire— not her exact words. Something about his total lack of either direction or ambition. Hearing this from his parents he could tune out. Hearing it from a hot brunette as he watched her fine behind departing his third-floor apartment for the last time, that was a bit harder to ignore.

He'd hopped on the Internet. And when he'd looked up fire—for lack of anything better to do—an image of wildfire had caught his attention. Somehow, that single glimpse had led to enrolling in a fire lookout certification course and quitting his job as a car mechanic.

"Now you've done it, buddy," Tom looked out at the view and decided that whether stupid, whimsical, or psychotic, it had been a damn fine decision—perhaps the first good one in his adult life.

He clamped his hands on the heavy wood rail and gave it a shake—not even a wiggle. His new home was as solid as the rock it stood on.

The Gray Wolf Summit lookout tower was perched at over seven thousand feet. The valleys fell away on three sides down to three thousand feet and then soared vertically back up, though few of the peaks reached his lofty height. To the north, the ridge descended less dramatically, giving him a long slope of hikeable terrain.

He'd never done much hiking, but couldn't wait to try it out. Per Forest Service training, he had his bear-sized can of pepper spray, supposedly the safest and most effective solution to stop a bear. Same size as a can of spray paint, it shot a cloud of pepper that was the most effective way to stop a charging bear—far better than a big gun, the numbers said. He still would have liked a big gun, but since he'd be as likely to shoot himself as the bear, he'd decided against it.

Beneath his boot soles, he stood on a planked walkway twenty-three feet above the rocky summit ridge; the true summit—a rounded crown of rock—lay fifty feet west and half as high as his tower. The forest fire lookout tower that would be his home for the next five months was a heavy wooden structure. Massive beams of rough-hewn dark wood formed the crisscross framework that supported the tower. Thirty-seven steps made of two-inch thick planks of Douglas fir led up to the fourteen-foot square glass-windowed "cab" that was now home. Those old Depression-era CCC guys really knew how to build something to last; most of the towers and lodges in the Pacific Northwest and Montana had been put up by those "back to work" crews.

He breathed in the air and held it as long as he could. He wanted to savor its taste, its clarity, the complete absence of any hint of civilization or old motor oil. He was so sick of all the people who thought their car was so darned important. It's a machine, people, use it, don't marry it. He was glad to be away from them.

He was almost as sick of them as he was of himself, which was really saying something.

The true extent of his aloneness he was less comfortable with.

Tom's next nearest neighbors were Tess and Jack on Cougar Peak lookout fifteen miles to the north, Swallow Hill twenty miles to the southwest, and—according to his radio plan—Old Crag equally far to the east.

Gray Wolf Summit wasn't on some through-trail, or a trail to anywhere at all except Gray Wolf Summit. It had been a long eight-mile hike with a gargantuan pack that had him cursing in the first mile as he crested a thousand-foot climb only to descend into an even deeper valley.

Vic, the Forest Service ranger in charge of the Selway-Bitterroot and Lolo lookouts, had warned him that his likely visitors over the summer would be the mule skinner who delivered the bulk of his supplies, his substitute who would come up for two days out of every two weeks, and one or two extreme fire-lookout tourists. Gray Wolf, perched at the end of a dead-end trail, was a brutal enough hike to discourage all except the most dedicated.

"Well," he told a turkey buzzard soaring on the high winds with its wing-tip feathers spread like fingers—the bird was probably the only one he'd be talking to most of the time. "If you're seeking something that died, you can cart off the Old Me."

He didn't know who he'd be by the end of the summer, that's why he was up here. But he knew he wasn't going to be the wandering soul who was presently standing on the lookout tower.

It was going to be an interesting summer.

2

*P*atty Dale hiked up the narrow trail. She'd been looking forward to this summer for four years now. Sure, it was the ass end of wildlife biology— first-year field work—but she didn't care. Being paid to tramp over the mountains and valleys of the Lolo for the next year was her idea of heaven.

She'd absolutely paid her dues.

"No one," her parents had told her, "no one does Army ROTC as a wildlife biologist." Her fellow cadets agreed, but she'd known what she wanted to do since the first reintroduced wolves were released into Yellowstone Park on her sixth birthday—March 21, 1995 after a seventy-year absence.

"Just watch me," though she'd said it only to herself at the time.

Now, after four years in the Army, she'd have said aloud, "Who the fuck do you think you are, judging my ass?"

Patty liked the self-confidence she'd learned in the military, though she was going to have to clean up her language—another gift of her military service—now that she was an academic, working for the Montana Fish, Wildlife & Parks.

An academic—first in her family past high school. First not to work in the open-pit copper mines of Butte, Montana. Busted flat when the operations closed down for several years in the '80s and again when she was in her teens. She was the only one to make it out.

Now, at twenty-six she'd done her time and survived her two full tours overseas. For the rest of her life, she would get to do what *she* wanted to. And right now that included hunting gray wolves—the largest of the wild canines—with a camera and a notebook.

It seemed cliché, but two wolf packs had bred in dens on the mid-level slopes to either side of Gray Wolf Summit. The chance to study two packs simultaneously was almost unheard of. Her rookie year was going to fucking rock…to seriously rock. Whatever.

Patty would be spending most of her time down in the forest, but the chance to sit on Gray Wolf Summit before she did was too perfect to pass up.

Shaded north sections of the trail were still covered with snow. Typical June in Montana. Portions of the mountains were still thick with winter, while in other sections the aspen and maple leafed out in a hundred shades of bright green. The dark spruce and Douglas fir grew bright fingertips at the end of every branch making the mountainside glow with new life.

She took her time hiking up the trail. Rabbit pellets and deer scat littered the trail here and there. Wolf tracks crossed the trail in a section just a half-mile long, this is where she'd start tomorrow. A single massive bear's paw print, in the mud close beside a racing stream of snowmelt runoff, was the first she'd ever seen on her own. She took a photo of it next to her own size six hiking boot. It would look great on her wall, if she ever got a place of her own.

Right now, home was a barracks in Helena, two hundred miles to the east. She didn't plan on being there much this year.

She filled her water bottles, dropped a purification tablet and an electrolyte packet into each one, resettled her pack, and continued up the trail.

Patty made it to the peak after full dark. The fire lookout tower was a blacked-out silhouette against the stars. She dropped her pack and sighed, glad to be free of the load. Using only the starlight, she rolled out an air mattress on the lichen and climbed into her sleeping bag on the very summit. She lay awake a long time after finishing an energy bar and an apple for dinner. Her contentment reached far and wide, watching her breath turn to mist before dissipating against a wilderness of stars.

She knew a lot of the constellations, but the old stories never seemed to fit. Well, now they had plenty of time to become friends. She had been planning to pick up a book, or at least one of those charts with the pretty drawings so that she'd really know the constellations by summer's end. Then she decided that she'd rather make up her own mythology, reinvent herself in the here and now.

She'd never really seen the big bear of Ursa Major in the Big Dipper. It was just a dipper. From now on, it would dedicated to her first drink of stream water now that she was free.

Hercules was high in the sky, a wasp-waisted group

of stars with a sword raised high. She renamed it Warrior Patty. Four years she'd fought for the U.S. Army. Before that she'd fought against the vortex of her family's history that had threatened to suck her down into the copper mine as well.

She fell asleep before she'd decided how to rename Cygnus the Swan flying up over the eastern horizon.

3

Tom woke in his lookout "cab" disoriented by the soft dawn light in such a foreign place. His body felt like he'd been battered by the night. The silence was so deep that his ears had rung loud enough to keep him awake. And no matter how deeply he tucked into his sleeping bag, he couldn't seem to get away from the cold.

And there had been the noises.

With the sunset, the world had gone silent, every bird asleep, his buddy the buzzard nesting somewhere in the trees far below. Not a breath of wind.

Then, he'd heard animals rustle about outside and imagined the worst. After a loud thump and strange, soft call like a sigh, there had been slick, snake-like sounds he couldn't identify. Torn between cold and fear, he'd decided that getting up to lock his front door situated at the top of thirty-seven stairs really wasn't necessary— not if he wanted to have any self-respect in the morning.

On the verge of getting up to lock it anyway, a wolf howl lifted into the night. He pictured a entire pack storming his tower if he made the slightest noise. The single cry was far off and left him awake and shivering for hours.

With large windows encircling his cabin in the sky—his tiny summer home was almost entirely glass from waist to head-high—the low sunlight was rapidly heating it up from sub-Arctic to toasty. Around the edges it had a bed, desk, two comfortable chairs, and a long worktable with a pair of stools facing an amazing view. The entire view was amazing. He could see no signs of civilization in any direction and he was above the whole forest.

Up above the wrap-around windows was an outlined drawing that was a map of the surrounding terrain and named every peak and valley for three-hundred-and-sixty degrees. In the center stood a raised cabinet topped by the Osborne Fire Finder for locating a burn if he saw one.

The first thing Tom did after crawling out of his sleeping bag was to pick up the big binoculars and scan the horizon and the trees for smoke. His training had made sure he remembered to look both near and far—to scan the nearby slopes as well as the distant peaks. The fire season didn't officially start for a few days and he knew that it could be weeks before he saw his first one, if he saw one at all.

Three-quarters of the way around, he yelped.

Smoke!

A huge plume of it.

Still holding the binoculars, he waved his other hand around reaching for his radio when he caught a view of something silver.

Tom peeked over the top of the binoculars, but

couldn't see any fire down toward Cougar Peak or in the valley directly below.

But the thing had been massive.

And then he looked closer.

A woman with light-colored hair was sitting cross-legged in front of a small fire that occasionally released a little puff of smoke. The flash of silver was a small cooking pot. Even as he watched, she tipped it into a mug and then dumped in a slim packet of—he adjusted the binoculars' focus—instant coffee.

He swung the glasses up to see her face…and she was looking right at him.

Okay, voyeuristic. He lowered the glasses and waved before it could become voyeuristic in a bad way. She didn't wave back.

He stepped out the door onto the walkway around the cab.

"Sorry," he called out. "I thought you were a forest fire."

"Well, that's a new one."

At just fifty feet away he could see she sat on a heavy field pack. She wore a thick jacket, messy light-brown hair ruffled down to her collar. Looking at her all wrapped up, he suddenly realized he was freezing his balls off. He looked down.

Briefs and binoculars.

"Holy crap!" he hurried back inside to the sound of her snort of amusement.

*a*bout the time Patty finished making her oatmeal in the same pot she'd made coffee, the lookout guy emerged again. This time he was wearing enough layers to look like the Michelin tire man.

Too bad. He'd looked good in just his tighty-whities. He wasn't macho-soldier strong, but he was close.

She'd done her best not to think about men since she'd gotten her commander court-martialed for thinking he could take liberties. It had led to her complete isolation by the men in the unit, and by the women as well—a lot of whom were screwing other soldiers, married and not. Totally gross.

Mr. Fire Lookout stood about six feet and didn't move down the stairs like an athlete or a soldier. He moved like a geek. Even though he now carried a mug of his own, he didn't approach her campfire until she waved him over.

Man unsure of himself. That was a new one. Most guys, especially the ones without a clue, moved with a self-entitled assuredness and bravado that only served to piss her off.

He moved close to the fire but didn't sit, instead looming above her. Well, she wasn't going to crick her neck for any male of the species.

"Sit down or shove off," she pulled out a squeeze bottle of maple syrup and drizzled a scant teaspoon on her oatmeal to make the syrup last.

"Sorry," he sat. So not a total write-off.

Patty hadn't really wanted company, but then again, she was the one who'd camped by a lookout tower—you get what you pay for. "Got a name?"

"Yes. Do you?"

She almost spewed her first mouthful of scalding oatmeal in his face along with her barely contained laughter.

Handsome unsure guy with a sense of humor?

"Sure," she kept eating and they shared a smile. "They're useful things to have…at times. I'll just call you Fireboy."

"Works for me." Still he didn't ask her name and she could no longer conveniently ask for his. Instead he sipped his coffee and stared out at the sunlight-etched shadows as sunrise moved across the tree-dark slopes.

This was why she'd come here, to watch daybreak sweep over the rugged mountains.

It certainly wasn't to be studying the profile of the man etched against the softening blue sky.

5

Tom stared into the distance and struggled for something to say. Though women didn't make him tongue-tied, he knew that he wasn't the smoothest guy around. Now Jimmy at the auto-body shop could talk female clients out of their BMWs and straight into a hotel room, but Tom had never figured out how.

But after convincing himself that he was alone in the wilderness, then flashing himself at a woman camping at the edge of a thousand foot drop-off, he didn't know what to say. She was pretty, at least her face and hair were. Her fingers were fine and strong. The rest of her was covered in a thick jacket, many-pocketed camo pants, and heavy hiking boots.

The women he knew were the sorts who wanted to hit a movie or go out drinking. Outdoorsy ones would play Frisbee on the lawn at Gasworks Park overlooking Lake Union and downtown Seattle.

This one was sitting on a pack that looked heavier than his had been and was cooking breakfast over an open campfire a dozen miles from the next nearest living soul.

"What brings you to Gray Wolf Summit?" That was safe enough, wasn't it?

"Exactly," she mumbled as she sucked in cool pine air over a hot mouthful of oatmeal. She didn't elaborate.

"You came for the summit?"

"No, the gray wolf part."

Was she naturally prickly or was she just teasing him? He decided to wait her out. After all, he'd felt plenty lonely last night—not knowing that an attractive woman was camped just a shout away—and it was only his first day in the wilderness. He didn't want to scare off what might be his only visitor for the entire summer.

"Wildlife biologist. I'm here to monitor the gray wolf dens off either side of the trail," she hooked a thumb back over her shoulder.

"They're here?" He spun to look, feeling as if one was about to attack him from behind. Nothing but the rolling line of the ridge, the narrow alpine meadow of grass and wildflowers with his wooden outhouse perched a few hundred feet downslope. Beyond that, the short scrub trees that eked out a living high on the granite, though their spareness quickly developed into a thick forest.

"Sure," she said, continuing to pay attention to her oatmeal and the distant mountains. "Plenty of trail sign if you'd known what to look for on your way up."

He could hear all of the points he'd just lost by missing the "shit signs." Like how was he supposed to know. Though drawings did fill the tiny safety handbook the Forest Service had given him during training.

"There are two known dens and we think they're

both occupied. I'm going to watch, record, set camera traps…all of the fun stuff." She'd finished off her breakfast and returned to her coffee.

"You don't look like a lunatic."

"Don't ask my former commander."

"Deal." Ex-military, which made the "lunatic" assessment even less likely. This was a woman with skills and a lack of fear because of those skills.

Whereas he had a complete lack of wilderness skills, which totally explained last night. Well, he wouldn't be letting himself go there again. From now on his fears would only be real ones.

"I'll just call you Wolfgirl."

"You're saying I'm not a woman?" No sense of offense, as if she was just asking.

"Wolfwoman doesn't exactly trip off the tongue. Besides, if I'm Fireboy, you're stuck with Wolfgirl."

"As long as you aren't calling me a bitch."

Female wolf. Bitch. "Don't know you well enough to decide one way or another."

"I'll be around. By the end of the summer, you'll know for sure that I am."

She'd be around.

He'd spent much of last night wondering if there was any way he could cut and run. Fire tower, isolation, howling wolves, the whole bit. Now, no more imaginary fears and, maybe, he wouldn't be so alone all summer.

A regular visitor.

He could deal with that.

Tom had settled into a semblance of routine after the first couple weeks. Up with the sun—he'd never been an early riser—but there wasn't much to do up here at night except watch the stars. First scan of the horizon for the day, then a couple-hour hike up and down the trail. Eventually, he'd branched off the trail for longer and longer forays through the pine and fir forest. He started seeing the "shit signs" but decided that unless they were still steaming he wasn't going to worry, too much. The one time he saw bear scat—freaking gigantic—he actually pulled his pepper spray can from his hip holster for the rest of that hike.

At first, he'd been hoping to run into Wolfgirl, but then he'd started noticing the wildlife and the plants changed with elevation along the trail. The Forest Service safety guide let him identify the basics, but he'd get a better guidebook on his first break back in town.

He was on duty from nine a.m. til six in the evening. He sent a morning radio report of weather readings and the fact that he was "in service." Every fifteen minutes, scan the horizon for "a smoke"—the little wisp of white that promised fire close behind. It was a little dizzying at times sweeping the binoculars up and down the hills— they went on forever. Once he got disoriented enough he couldn't remember where he'd started and had to go around a second time. After that he started and ended with due north.

Due north was the trail that Wolfgirl had walked down two weeks ago, swinging her monstrous backpack on as if it weighed nothing at all.

He felt better when he noticed that she too carried the bear spray rather than a gun. She was a wildlife biologist, so he'd guess that she knew what was best. And being a soldier meant that she had a handgun skill set that he didn't.

When she'd stood up, she'd been smaller than he'd expected. Somehow a person who tracked over the wilderness fearlessly seeking a massive four-legged predator should stand more than five-foot six. His final view of her had been a single pair of slender, camo-clad legs sticking out from below her pack and a battered blue baseball cap with a Montana State University bobcat logo above.

After two weeks—and still no sign of Wolfgirl—he'd had his first two days "down." A lookout relief had hiked in and continued the firewatch while he got off the mountain and went into town—a four-hour hike out and another hour skidding his car down muddy logging roads and then the bland pavement of the highway to Missoula. A night at the bar and crashing in a cheap motel. Alone.

There'd been a couple of potentials at the bar, but he wasn't into it. He'd had his fair share of cheap sex—

it usually cost a couple beers, some nachos, and a little dancing. It had always bothered him that the dancing was often better than the cheap sex.

He hadn't felt that way at first, of course. Women in bars had started happening for him as he'd shifted from geeky academic to muscled mechanic from wrenching on crumpled car frames all day. It was true, macho guys got the hot women and he'd certainly enjoyed the benefits of that at first. But now, his ego didn't need the boost and he just didn't care for the hollow feeling morning-afters always left.

Technically, he had another day down. Instead, he hit the bookstore for a wilderness guide. *Flora and Fauna of the Lolo Forest* was perfect. Then he spotted a title on wolves and grabbed it too. It had become clear that Wolfgirl was gone from his life, but he wanted to read up on them anyway. Tom went through the grocery store, loaded up his pack to a ridiculous weight, and struggled back up to the summit.

And Wolfgirl had left him a note with the substitute lookout.

Hi! and a line-drawing of what he now recognized as a wolf's paw print for a signature. Later that afternoon, he'd been idly doodling between lookout duties, and had drawn wind-blown hair around the paw print as if it was a face.

He didn't know why it mattered, but it did.
Shit!

It was late afternoon and Patty should have headed down the trail and into town. She hated to be away from the mountain and her wolf dens. There were two packs. One pack of six had a dozen pups just starting to peek their noses out of the dens. The other was a threesome led by a great, black-furred male; the smaller pack had just five pups as far as she could tell. The two groups had very little to do with each other except for the older female of the threesome, gray in the muzzle, who hunted across the range. It was her tracks that crossed the trail back and forth. All the other wolves hunted down the valleys on their own sides of the ridge.

Patty had spent three intense weeks trying to track that lone female and discover what she was doing on both sides, but hadn't found out yet. Patty monitored the packs nonstop, except for an afternoon, going up to the lookout tower, only to discover that was Fireboy's day off the mountain.

Quite what had drawn her up the mountain that day

was unclear. She'd only shared a cup of coffee and a few jokes, but he'd stuck in her mind. One thing she'd learned in the Army was to pay attention to those little things. In Iraq, wondering about that unexplained cardboard box along the roadside, could be someone's groceries, could be an IED. Don't remember that pile of cut wheat stalks off the side of the road at the junction? Turns out to be perfect cover for a shooter.

Now she was back again, to find out what had stuck in her mind about Fireboy. She thought about kicking the timber at ground-level a couple of times to announce she was coming. Then she remembered his seriously cute, "Holy crap!" when he'd discovered he wasn't wearing anything but very tight briefs and binoculars.

Patty kept her gait light on the stairs and moved upward silently despite her heavy pack which had become like a second skin. On the way up, she could only marvel at the view after having her head down in the woods for three weeks. She so loved being out here.

Up at the catwalk level, she could see through the broad windows into the cabin—it was a very fine view indeed. He was wearing shorts, but that was all. It was June 21st according to her observations log book, mid-summer's eve, and the late afternoon sun was warm.

The stairs had landed her at the north side, close beside the door. Fireboy was facing away from her doing a slow methodical scan of the hills to the south. Now only ten feet away, she could see the definition of his shoulder muscles put on display by his raised arms.

Clean, no tats, like a canvas not yet written upon. Beneath her shirt she wore a lone she-wolf face on her left shoulder blade. Eyes closed, howling a song of purest joy.

He slowly turned in her direction as he inspected his way around the hills. The abs definition from the side was just as nice.

Then facing her…and finally the fat end of the binocs lined up on her face and she smiled.

"Holy crap!" just like the first time. He jerked down the glasses and looked at her blankly.

She didn't know what response she wanted or expected from him. But it was a good one when it came—

"Wolfgirl!" His smile was huge and welcoming. Then he raised the binoculars again and got points for not aiming them at her breasts. "My, what big teeth you have."

Patty laughed. It was something she hadn't done in a long time. Not since before her commander had almost succeeded in raping her—"because deep down she really wanted it"—before she succeeded in breaking his face—"because deep down he really wanted it." Not since…she didn't know when.

8

<hr>

om was glad it was the end of the afternoon watch, his last scan of the peaks and valleys for the day. She was actually here, standing in his doorway as if that was somehow completely normal. Only habit reminded him to call in an end-of-day report of "no smokes, no fire activity, Gray Wolf Summit out of service."

He thought about all of the clichés. "You're here!" "Wasn't expecting you!" Really wasn't.

He also hadn't known quite how beautiful she was. He'd seen her face before, clear skin, dark eyes of unfathomable depth. Even in the three weeks since he'd last seen her, her hair had grown and now looking just a little out of control, a touch wild. She was what the guys at the shop would have called a "solid gal." Not heavy—there was not an ounce of heavy anywhere on Wolfgirl—but not slender or model frail either. She was the kind of woman who had the strength to do something other than look good in clothes. The chest and waist belts of her pack stretched

66

her thin cotton T-shirt tight over her breasts. Very nice.

Say something you idiot!

"Was that you I heard howling at the moon last night?"

"Might have," that grin lit up her face even brighter.

Forget pretty, plug in gorgeous with that smile.

"Catch any fires yet?" she asked.

He slapped a hand tragically to his chest, and realized that once again he was mostly unclothed in front of her. *Go with it.* "Not so much as a firefly," he moaned like a player in a Shakespearean drama.

"Not much of a Fireboy, are you?"

He tried to sigh tragically.

Must have worked; that surprising, musical laugh reemerged.

"How goes the wolf hunt?" he wanted to keep her talking.

"Fucking awesome!"

"Drop your pack..." *please stay awhile,* "...and tell me."

She did, dropping it with a heavy thunk that seemed to shake the cab with its weight. She pulled out a water bottle and turned to point north.

Then she cursed, "Do you have a map?"

Now it was his turn to laugh. There was the drawing around the whole top of the wall. There was the wide area map mounted on the Osborne finder that gave him the area for fifty miles in every direction. And on the main desk he kept a 7-1/2-minute quadrangle map rolled out. It showed the area for seven-and-a-half miles north of Cougar Peak—the area he'd known she was tramping.

"Do you have the fifteen?"

He pulled out the larger area 15-minute map.

For the next half hour she led him on a tour of a vast range of hills and valleys, amazing him with the amount of territory she and the wolves covered. Her hard-bitten nails tracing the lines of brutal climbs that had nothing to do with fire-tower trails or logging roads. She'd been hiking straight through brush. The excitement in her voice was so true and pure and it evoked a whole series of emotions.

At first, awe that anyone could care so much about…anything. She was pulling out her log book to trace the wolves' movements more accurately over the terrain of the map.

Then it was discomfort and finally a shame that had him shuffling foot to foot. He cared about nothing this much; the past few years he'd mostly felt…just blank.

What the hell was he doing with his life?

A college degree he couldn't imagine ever using, a career that included wiping blood, vomit, and empty beer bottles out of shattered cars before he could even work on them, and now sitting alone watching a forest that might never catch on fire. Even if it did, the more experienced spotters at Cougar Peak or Old Crag would probably spot it long before he did.

But finally Wolfgirl overwhelmed his sense of uselessness. Her excitement swept him aboard.

When she spotted Dutcher and Dutcher's *The Hidden Life of Wolves* on his desk, she cried for joy and dragged it onto the map to flip pages searching for pictures that would show him what The Messenger—as she'd dubbed the traveling female—looked like. He'd barely been able to focus on the pictures as they rubbed shoulders and jostled together hip to hip while she told more stories.

He'd made dinner, that she'd bolted, and they'd made love on his narrow bunk as the sunset filled the fire tower with the colors of fire. She rose over him, feral, powerful, as wild as her wolves. The red-gold light played over her skin as she threw her head back and cried out when he sheathed himself and entered her.

Tom half expected her to howl, instead she groaned like her heart had been ripped from her chest. He leaned up to bury his lips and his face between her breasts and she pulled him in with a truth, with an honesty of emotion he'd never found in a woman before.

This was not a woman who revved his engines or fit him like the seat of a Porsche 944 Turbo. She was too primal, too purely herself for that.

When their climaxes ripped through them he felt every jolt through her body as if it was his own.

And after their pulses peaked then slowed and their bodies both shuddered until she finally lay still upon his chest, then she wept.

He held her, stroked her hair, and whispered in her ear that she was okay.

Okay? She was life-changing amazing, but that wasn't what she needed to hear right now as the sobs wracked her, as the smell of salt tears washing against his cheek threatened to overpower the scent of the forest that clung to her hair.

They slept clinging tightly to each other.

In the middle of the night, she woke him, and by the light of the stars she lay beneath him and they were as gentle with each other as they'd been frantic earlier.

Tom woke alone with the sunlight streaming over him.

A note rested on the open page of *The Hidden Lives of Wolves.*

> *I owe you three pounds of oatmeal,*
> *a half bottle of maple syrup,*
> *and a box of energy bars.*
> *You're very pretty when you sleep.*

AGAIN, the paw-print signature.

This time there was a radio frequency.

She'd left the note on the picture of the wolf he'd chosen as prettiest in the whole book. It was a close-up of black-furred wolf. Just her face, with her chin resting on the snow, yellow eyes looking right at the camera.

9

*P*atty went back to him whenever she could tear herself away.

Talked to him by radio on other nights when he wasn't on fire watch and the wolves weren't on an active hunt.

June passed into July.

Fireboy's first fire sighting had them talking for hours over their radios. She normally limited herself to fifteen minutes to conserve batteries, but he'd been so excited she couldn't help herself and let him roll. She'd been very attentive the next day to make sure that her solar battery charger was always aligned to best advantage to the sun.

Something was changing inside her. Patty had come to the wilderness for her wolves and the silence of nature, but like a bear to a honey trap, she couldn't resist circling back to the fire tower atop Gray Wolf Summit.

It wasn't even the sex.

Okay. It wasn't just the sex.

When they were, nothing else existed. There were

visits when they hardly spoke a word. She would track him to his cabin atop the summit, take all he could give her, sleep in his arms, and be gone back to the wolves by daybreak. Such a heavy sleeper, he rarely woke to see her off. But when he did, he always caressed her gently and kissed her sweetly. One of those wordless nights he'd spent hours tracing every line of her wolf tattoo as if stamping its joy onto her soul more deeply than the tattoo artist had.

Other visits, they might not make love at all. Just watch the sunset, curl up in each other's arms, and sleep. They talked of nothing and everything, but only about the present. Neither of them had a past or future. Neither of them even had a name.

Patty was not her mother or her grandmother or even her great-gran. They had all married their men at sixteen or seventeen and given birth well before the acceptable nine months had passed.

The one thing Patty knew for certain, being with a man for more than a time or two was too great a risk. Too dangerous. But again that bear to the honey trap; she could no more resist Fireboy than he could her.

He'd taken to doing the town food-run for both of them so that she didn't have to leave the wilderness. On his way down the mountain, he would radio, gather what little trash she couldn't burn, and bring back an extra twenty pounds of supplies. He never stayed away overnight, though she never let him return directly to the tower unrewarded.

If the wolves were running that night, she'd sneak him into one of the blinds she'd created along the primary trail. He'd been nervous as hell the first couple times, even after she assured him that wolves didn't attack humans. But as they watched The Messenger through the view screen on her night-vision camera—and the female had given them little more than a sideways glance—he'd settled down. When the wolf was gone, they made love among the soft ferns with the rich smell of the forest duff wrapped around them.

"Wolfgirl!" the radio snapped at her early on a hot August afternoon.

A startled rabbit leapt and bolted from close beside Patty's position.

The Messenger shot after it, but Patty knew the wolf would be too late.

"What?" she yelled back into the radio.

"Where are you?"

"Go away!" She began gathering her camera gear and was about to shut off the radio in frustration—the rabbit would have made a great catch and she knew how hard it was getting for the old wolf to hunt. This wouldn't be her last season, but the end had just come a little closer.

"Where are you? It's important," he shouted at her.

"Head of Long Tail Creek, about two hundred yards above the western den."

"You need to get out of there. Get up onto the ridge trail. Either get to me or get off the mountain."

"Why?" But she heard why. She found a break in the forest canopy and caught a glimpse of a black airplane painted with orange-and-red flames like a sports car. Even as she watched, small figures dressed in yellow tumbled out of the rear and then popped open parachutes.

Two smokejumpers. Four.

The plane circled back, four more.

And a third time.

Two smokejumpers is what they sent to stop a typical small fire, under an acre. Four could beat down a half dozen acres. A dozen smokies was very bad news indeed.

A helicopter came in. Instead of delivering more smokejumpers up high, it came in so low that she had to cover her ears as it by passed overhead and continued down into the steep valley. Then there was a high whine, momentarily louder than the roaring engines and the pounding rotors, and a shower of red retardant sheeted from the sky down onto the forest in the valley far below her—but not that far.

The wind, almost undetectable down here in the trees, was brushing downslope, which would explain why she hadn't smelled any wood smoke. Even though the wind might be washing down the hill, fire loved to climb.

Patty was a dozen scrambling steps upslope before she caught herself.

The Messenger hadn't smelled the wood smoke either. And if she hadn't, then the wolves in the den down below hadn't.

It was absurd, she was human, they were wolves. But she knew them, had named and cataloged each one, knew them by their markings, their behaviors, even the half-grown pups. Of them all, only The Messenger remained nameless to her.

Another helo roared by low overhead, another sheet of red cascading from the sky.

"Wolfgirl, tell me you're on the move."

She wasn't. She was frozen between escape and saving—

Patty plunged down the slope, smashing a shoulder against a tree to slow herself down when her speed went out of control, jumping over a boulder that threatened to kneecap her and landing a dozen feet below in a roll that was only broken when she tumbled into a blackberry patch. Cursing and bleeding from a dozen scratches, she circled wide below the den.

The roar of chainsaws and heart-stopping thunder of crashing trees below told that the trouble was far closer than she'd like.

Approach the den from below.

The pack was out front, agitated by the noise, but not frightened by the fire they couldn't smell. Blackthorne the big male pacing back and forth. Mariko, the small pack's second female—Blackthorne's true love in *Shogun*—was guarding the pups, keeping them confined in the cave.

Patty climbed back toward them.

"Shoo! Move!" The massive black pack leader turned to face her but, other than a worried snarl, made no effort to move off. She didn't dare move any closer, he might attack her in simple panic. Then she had an idea.

Patty pulled out her can of bear pepper spray. She shot the smallest squirt she could upslope and a bit to the side.

She heard a sharp *Yip!* from Blackthorne just as she realized her mistake. The rising heat of the fire below them was now actively pulling air downslope to feed itself. The pepper spray she'd shot near the wolf was also dragged right back down on her.

It wafted into her face.

She cried out in pain as it hit her eyes and nostrils

despite her raised arm. Diving down, she rubbed her face in the soft ferns and cool earth. She screamed out the pain that even that small amount of spray had caused.

When she could finally see again, Blackthorne was gone. The female was following and several bushy-tailed youngsters disappeared with them into the brush—upslope, thank god.

She couldn't count how many pups through her streaming eyes, so she forced her way up to the den. A lone twenty-pound pup had been left behind, Vasco by his markings—one white ear, one black—the Portuguese pilot and Blackthorne's lone friend. So terrified that he didn't even nip at her as she reached in to drag him out.

Patty struggled up the steep slope.

What had been a crashing three-minute descent became a brutal half-hour climb. She tried releasing Vasco, dropping him to the ground and shooing him upwards but he merely cowered at her feet, front paw raised. She saw it had a nasty cut and probably hurt too much to walk on. It would heal in the den, could be ignored in a three-footed run across level ground, but the pup couldn't climb a steep slope with it.

She eventually became aware of two things.

The rising heat wasn't only from her hard climb, the fire was starting to run up the narrow cleft.

The other thing was Fireboy's near frantic calls.

"I'm headed upslope," she answered in between raged gasps. "I have an injured pup. But the fire's close. It's hot."

"God damn it, Wolfgirl. Drop it and run!"

She knew that was the smart thing, the wise thing

but, "I can't," her voice came out as a sob and she kept struggling up the slope.

As she climbed past where the initial radio call had spooked the rabbit and The Messenger, she started scanning for the female. There was no question, she would know to run. Wouldn't she? Patty hadn't.

There was still no smell of smoke, just the insufferable heat.

Patty continued battling her way through the brush. The slope rose so steeply that her sore knee—she must have cracked it against something during her pell-mell descent—often banged against tree roots and rocks.

Would the wolf pup tolerate being inside a fire shelter with her? She doubted it, but they might have no choice.

That's when she noticed her pack was gone. She'd shed it somewhere. Her camera, data, and radio were attached to her fanny pack, but all of her clothes and gear were lost somewhere in the trees and boulders. And in it was the foil fire shelter kept for true, last-resort emergencies.

A glance back over her shoulder was a bad mistake. The fire had reached the den, only three hundred yards below her, but with flames reaching hundreds of feet above the hundred-foot tall trees. Even glancing over her shoulder, the heat was a slap on the face. And the roar, the roar was deafening.

There might have been a radio call, but she couldn't hear it over the fire's howl.

She turned and kept climbing though her knee throbbed at every step. The stitch in her side was so bad that she was almost weeping into the wolf pup's fur. Every step had become agony.

Bear down, soldier! There is no such thing as quitting!

She bore down, but she didn't have much to bear down with.

The roar and the wind peaked, slamming against her so hard that all she could do was drop to her knees and wait for it.

"Hi."

Patty screamed as a hand touched her on the shoulder.

A man clad in yellow Nomex and a pilot's helmet dangled at the end of a wire not a foot from her.

Patty's gaze followed the wire upward until she spotted the helicopter hovering high above the trees, its engines even louder than the fire, the downblast shaking trees and brush.

"Steve Mercer, Mount Hood Aviation. How about we get out of here?"

She held the wolf pup closer, "I'm not leaving Vasco."

The man swept the pup under one arm—Vasco whined nervously but accepted the transfer—and twisted a lifting ring toward her. It was also attached to the wire; he held it so that the opening faced Patty.

It was like a circular orange life preserver.

"Head, arms, and shoulders through the hole," he instructed as calmly as if they were on a quiet street corner. "Keep your arms down so that it catches you in the armpits. Keeping them down locks you in place."

She did as he said and moments later they were lifting up out of the trees, spinning slowly, too much like a rotisserie in the approaching fire's heat.

Once they were clear of the trees, the helo pulled them away from the fire and she could start to breathe again. A hundred feet above the trees, the flames still reached far higher, but they were rapidly falling astern as they continued to climb up the slope.

"Emily says that we'll drop you at the base of the mountain," the man shouted to her.

"Can you drop us near the top?"

---

*P*atty curled up on the fire tower's bunk and tended the wolf pup. Calming the young wolf let her not think about how her eyes still stung, how much her knee hurt, or quite how close she'd come to dying.

She listened as Fireboy worked the radio through the long afternoon.

The smokejumpers fought the fire in pitched battle until it was trapped and couldn't spread either way along the valley wall. The helicopters had contained it before it crossed the ridge. The second den would be safe.

If The Messenger lived, perhaps she'd guide Blackthorne's pack over to join the larger one to the east.

She buried her face in Vasco's fur and wept for only the second time since that day as a young girl when she had understood the trap that her family was in. It was the day she'd determined to find a way out.

Patty had wept that first time in Fireboy's arms as

some impossible sense of loss had overwhelmed her, even if she hadn't known what the loss had been. And now she wept because she understood that from the first time with him, what she had left behind was the Warrior Girl fighting for freedom against all odds. In his powerful arms, she was more truly herself than anywhere she'd ever been.

A long time later, Fireboy sat down close beside her, but didn't touch her.

The sun had gone, but she hadn't noticed.

"Is it out?" her voice was rough and still stung from the pepper spray she'd inhaled.

"Yes," he nodded in the soft light of the small oil lamp that he'd lit. "A ground team has arrived and is making sure it stays dead. The smokies are already being lifted out by the helos. We have another fire north of Cougar Peak that they're needed on. How's the pup?"

She held up the long and sharp stone sliver that she'd extracted from Vasco's pad, "He'll heal fine now."

"Is he like a permanent addition to the family?"

"No, I can probably reintroduce him to his pack tomorrow. I think I know where they've moved to." And Patty knew she'd find The Messenger there, she just had to.

Then his words registered.

"The family?"

He shrugged easily, "Does seem to be what I said."

As she watched his face shifted. One moment he was casual, keeping up a cool façade. The next was a wash of emotion she couldn't even recognize, but both his hands were crushing down on one of hers.

"I thought I'd lost you. I've never been so afraid in my life. I couldn't imagine this world without you in it.

To never be able to talk to you again, laugh with you again, it simply wasn't possible, but it felt so real. I could barely help on the fire until they found you."

"Family?" she couldn't seem to get past the word. Was family about something more than mere survival? Hers had never been.

But she could see in his eyes that she did mean the world to him. She didn't need his crushing grip nor his eyes glistening in the soft lamplight to know that he'd been afraid to the very core. For her. Of losing her.

"I've never been important to anyone," Patty told him. "Not that important."

"I swear I almost went charging down into the fire myself to find you. If that Mount Hood Aviation helo hadn't called that they had you, I would have. I never knew what was important—that anything *could be* that important to me—until I met you."

And she could see the truth of that. He really would have run right into the fire for her.

The strange thing was, she'd have done the same for him. Without knowing how it happened, she'd discovered what family was supposed to be. It wasn't about surviving together, it was about helping each other. Not just from a fire, but from the heart.

She raised her free hand—the one not still locked in his crushing grip—from the pup's fur and brushed it over his cheek. How could she describe how she felt about him? How could she explain anything to someone who made her feel so important, so precious?

She leaned forward to kiss him lightly on the lips and then leaned back to look him in the eyes.

"Patty Dale," she whispered because what could be more important than a name.

"Tom Cunningham."

She listened to her heart and knew. Knew that this was simply right. As nothing in her life had ever been, even more than wildlife biology.

"Patty Cunningham?" She asked it softly, as much of herself as of him.

His smile was all the answer she needed.

BLAZE ATOP SWALLOW HILL LOOKOUT

Marta Chavez *possesses the dubious honor of spotting the most fires in a single season from her perch high atop Swallow Hill in Idaho's rugged Bitterroot Wilderness.*

Her fantasies of finding a decent man feel as ephemeral as wildfire smoke.

Until **Tyler Brown** *crash lands his firefighting helicopter at her remote cloister and they both must survive the Blaze Atop Swallow Hill Lookout.*

Many of my stories have odd little side connections (they're fun and I can't help myself). Though this one more than most.

Having placed a man among the peaks in the prior lookout story, I decided to place a woman there next. Marta has an uncle named Manuel who is a prominent character in my Where Dreams series. His and Graziella's story is spread across several of the titles, but lies mostly in *Where Dreams Reside* (Where Dreams #2).

But who should Marta fall in love with? A fire lookout tower is a remote and lonely spot, especially deep in the Idaho's Bitterroot Wilderness. Not exactly the best place for finding true love.

Hmmm…

Then I thought about the origin of the series, it came out of Firehawks, which is all about the helicopter pilots. And, of course, helicopter pilots often know other helicopter pilots and I had just finished the seventh novel in my Night Stalkers series, *By Break of Day*. So, the fans of that series may recognize Tyler's "Texas friend with a horse ranch" as Justin Roberts, the hero of *By Break of Day*.

Any lookout who has been in their tower when there is a firefight occurring nearby, talks about watching the "air show"—the aerial battle to contain and kill a wildfire.

But what happens when the fire gets a little *too* close to the fire lookout who spotted the flames?

Well, that's the story.

1

The "airshow" was spectacular, from a distance.

Marta Chavez scanned the horizon every fifteen minutes like a responsible fire lookout. But she spent the rest of her time watching the firefight over at Gray Wolf Summit, about twenty miles to the northeast of her tower. They were deep in the Lolo wilderness, rougher than Colorado, and only Alaska was more wild.

First the smokies had spilled out of the sky, their parachutes blooming and dancing about in the fire-driven winds. Then the new four-jet BAe 146 tanker had arrived on the fire, dropping great swaths of dark red retardant. A half dozen helos zipped through the air: a trio of the big converted Black Hawk helicopters called Firehawks that were at least as impressive as the BAe 146, and a second trio of little MD500s that flitted about the sky.

She always loved watching the MD500s. They only carried a little water, a hundred and thirty gallons versus the thousand of the Firehawk or the three thousand dropped by the BAe, but they could slip right up to a spot fire, blast it out of existence, and dance out of the way with a tight pirouette. It always reminded her of her childhood dreams of being a ballerina, dashed by the advent of breasts at the age of thirteen. Ballerinas were supposed to be willowy—even better if you were short and willowy.

Marta was tall and had ended up…very not willowy. Her mama had always said it was God's will; personally, Marta felt gypped.

So she'd gone out for track instead and that had led to cross-country, which was nuts for a woman with curves, but a doubled-up sports bra had cured the worst of that—still her chest hurt like the Madonna after some of the bigger runs.

Ultimately, running along the forest trails and logging roads of Coeur d'Alene, Idaho had led to a summer job as a fire lookout. Now she could watch helicopters dance so lightly on the winds that they reminded her that she wasn't so graceful. But still she couldn't stop watching them; her arms ached from holding the binoculars aloft even though her elbows were propped on the edge of her cabin's table.

It was the eighth fire she'd found already this summer, which earned her the dubious honor of being the number one spotter this season. She was just glad that none of them had been anywhere near her. The airshow must have really rattled Gray Wolf's cage as this fire burned right at the base of his lookout tower's mountain; which explained why she'd spotted it first—he'd had no view straight down off his cliff. They had it contained now; ground crews would be in to kill it in the morning. He'd never been threatened, but it could have gone bad.

Marta scanned the thickly-clad conifer mountains of the Lolo National Forest. Her first year she'd thought of it in mountains: Goat, White, Cougar. Now in her second season she knew it by the dark slashes of recent fires or the bright green of new growth after last season's: Colgate, Crazy Creek, Loco, and all the rest.

She finished the round, her last of the day, and called it in, "Swallow Hill reporting, no fires except Wolf's Den. Out of service."

"Roger that, Swallow Hill. Well done today." She liked Vic, the U.S. Forest Service ranger in charge of this sector. He always had something nice to say. She'd carried quite a fantasy about him during the first season…until she'd found out he was forty with a gut and married. But he had one of those deep, smooth voices.

Just like Helo 41. She could listen to Tyler, 41's lone pilot, report vectors and drops of his MD500 all day— he had a liquid Colorado accent, overly polite with just the sweetest hint of cowboy. But quite why a girl from Coeur d'Alene would swoon over such a thing—she'd never even been to Colorado. Didn't even know what he looked like, but she did enjoy listening to that voice of his.

Even though the official day of 9 a.m. to 6 p.m. was over for the lookouts, she kept both her radio and her scanner on as she made dinner. On the radio she heard Gray Wolf still working the communications with the ground crew. In the deep canyons of the Lolo, it was common that one ground crew couldn't talk to another, so the lookout tower would act as a relay.

She took her water jug down to the cistern and filled it up. The rainwater off her lookout tower roof had been collected throughout the winter into a concrete cistern built beneath her lookout tower on Swallow Hill. Hill—that just wasn't right. Swallow Hill might not be one of the big peaks—Cougar ruled the area up at almost nine thousand feet—but at seventy-five hundred, her "Hill" should have been respected as a mountain. She often felt sorry for it.

"We'll show 'em, girl," she patted the rock at the base of the steps before climbing back up toward the lookout's cabin.

The lookout tower itself was new, as far as lookout towers went. Most had been built by the Depression-era crews almost a century ago. Swallow Hill had been burned over in the sixties and had to be replaced. Rather than the elegance of one of the CCC's massive wooden structures, her tower was five stories of steel lattice. It had been built tall so that the view would be clear when the timber regrew. Fifty years after the burnover and the tallest trees were still only a dozen feet high. Most of the upper slope was lush alpine meadow. It gave her an amazing view from her twelve-foot square cab at the top.

A hundred and forty-four square feet of pure functionality. A two-foot wide "deck" wrapped all of the way around so that she could open and close the big shutters at the beginning and end of the season, and could clean the wrap-around glass windows in between.

Everything in its place, because if it wasn't, she'd trip on it. Dad's fifth-wheel camper was bigger than this place, and that was before he opened the slide-outs. The cab's center was dominated by the two-foot diameter disk of the Osborne Fire Finder to let her pinpoint a blaze. Around the perimeter was a chair, a cot, and a strip of counter that was desk, workbench, and kitchen. The cooler sat underneath the counter along with her pack and all of her dry groceries. Finding a spot for both her running shoes and her boots had been a problem until she'd decided to always keep one or the other on while she was awake.

She liked the contrast to her own room in her parents' home. She was only in Coeur d'Alene for the month between the fire and ski seasons, plus two days off every other week. But it was her childhood room. A dense clutter of kid projects, high school trophies, and a ton of crap she always meant to shed but could never quite bring herself to do, crowded the room impossibly. The only way to make her bed at home was to be on it.

Here she was neat as a pin; a different person. Here she wasn't six inches taller than any of her siblings. Here every guy on the block didn't know her, cat calling every time she went out for a run. Swallow Hill Lookout was just the watching and the silence. A golden eagle circled high on the wind above the cab; silent and shining in the low sunlight. A swallow swooped busily in and out of the swallow box she'd packed in this spring and attached to the steel trestle. It was ridiculous to have no swallows on Swallow Hill, and they hadn't nested among the sparse trees last season.

She'd been very cheered when the pair of swallows had claimed the box and begun nest building in it. The first tiny *cheep* sounding from the box's small round hole had been an almost transcendental experience. She'd rushed up and down the five-story trestle between every fifteen minute scan of the horizon…and barely been able to walk the next day her legs were so sore.

The young had only fledged yesterday, making the

terrifyingly heroic flight from bird box to the opposite side of the trestle, and then back to the bird box. By evening parents and children were soaring wild loops around the lookout tower clearing the air of any bugs foolish enough to brave the cool evening. The golden eagle had surveyed the quick and tiny swallows, as well as Marta herself, carefully. Apparently deciding that neither of them would make a tasty meal, she'd soared off seeking lusher pickings.

Marta waved at the flitting swallows then ducked into the cab and began boiling the water on her small gas stove. She was a third-generation Idahoan of Mexican descent with a taste for Italian food that she cultivated at her uncle's knee; Mama's much younger brother was often more her big brother than the two that Mama had provided her with. That was before Uncle Manuel had moved to Seattle to become a big time chef with an elegantly slender Italian wife. Graziella's problem was that she was so nice that Marta couldn't even hold being willowy against her. They'd become like sisters—which Marta had always wanted— both were dusky skinned…and that was the only part of their features that were in common.

While the water boiled, which took a while at this altitude, she flicked on the radio scanner, and began chopping sun-dried tomatoes and olives. The scanner gave her the bigger picture of what was happening in the area. Her radio was tuned only to the primary Forest Service frequency, but a lot went on among the heights of the Lolo National Forest and the Bitterroot-Selway Wilderness.

Last summer Tess Weaver and Jack Parker had done a whole courtship thing on a higher frequency. It had started out as radio chess, something that Marta was good enough at that she could generally follow their games without a board. When their conversations had shifted to more personal matters, she'd tuned off their frequency to give them a little privacy.

This season it was Tom up on Gray Wolf and some wildlife biologist following wolves. The discussions about wolves had been fascinating, but then they too had gotten all mushy and personal, and she'd taken to skipping their "private" frequency. Because of that she'd missed most of a rather dangerous rescue this afternoon when they'd had to use a helicopter to short-haul the biologist to safety.

There was no privacy on mountain radio, but each lookout extended the courtesy of pretending not to listen. Otherwise it became a very long and lonely season. Marta often traded recipes with Angeline up on Old Crag and with Jack on Cougar because Tess couldn't cook soup.

Marta tossed in the pasta, then diced in what she could salvage of her carrots and rather sad small zucchini. It was getting close to her bi-weekly resupply trip off the mountain and, with no refrigeration, veggies were scarce at the moment.

The airwaves were quiet tonight, except for the last of the airshow still going on around Gray Wolf Summit. They were down to the Incident Air Commander flying an airplane well above the fire for a good view and the big Firehawks laying down the main strikes. Tyler ducked his MD500 in and out of the fray with smooth precision.

She always waited for those moments. He never replied to a drop command with a simple, "Roger."

That would be too impolite for his breeding and his sense of humor.

"That little ol' spot? Why it's hardly a fire a-tall. You sure I should be snuffing her out? If I do, she'll never grow up all tall and proper like."

She could feel the ICA rolling his eyes somewhere far above. "Just hit the damn thing, Tyler."

"Yes sir. Your order is this flyboy's command. Just checking was all." And then he'd hammer it with perfect precision and turn back for the next load of water or retardant.

With her luck, he probably looked like a toad. Not that she'd ever meet him. Still, didn't hurt a girl to dream a little bit.

She served up her bowl of pasta and blanched veggies, sprinkled on the olives and sun-dried tomatoes, drizzling it with the oil from the tomatoes, and shaved the last of her precious Parmigiano-Reggiano cheese on it. She raised a small glass of red wine to the west in a salute to her uncle and the fair Graziella. It was just box wine, but it was the best she could offer—glass bottles weighed far too much to pack in both directions as Swallow Hill Lookout was six steep miles beyond the closest parking spot.

2

"No, Mom. I like my job," Marta growled at the first squirrel to peek around a young spruce tree to see who was starting up the long trail to the peak of Swallow Hill.

"I like my winter job too," she told an overly curious robin. Ski season she worked at the Silver Mountain Resort as a waitress. "Free lift tickets and next season they'll let me try out for ski patrol." Which would pay worse due to lack of tips, but irritate her much less. "I know it's not Schweitzer," the premier resort of Northern Idaho.

The robin flew off deciding that she didn't want anything to do with this half-mad lunatic. It happened to Marta every time she came off the mountain during the season. She reverted into some form of her normal self that she wasn't real happy with. And Mama had been on a roll because "that Janson girl just married your old flame the Malcolm boy."

"She's welcome to him," Marta told a garter snake, a big one almost two feet long. It scowled at her from its sunny rock where the trail turned to avoid an old slide that had taken down several alders and a six-inch maple. The alders, typically were doing well, the maple was turning back into mulch. The "Malcolm boy" had been good enough in bed, an event she had made sure Mama never knew about, but about as mentally exciting as watching paint dry, which fit for a housepainter. Of course "that Janson girl" hadn't been the brightest color in the palette either, so maybe it worked for her.

"I know I won't meet a man on the tops of mountains," she shouted at the snake when he flicked out a long red and black-tipped tongue at her. As she was neither a predator nor rational, he returned to enjoying his sun-warmed rock.

It was a problem, but it wasn't one she was terribly worried about. No one came up Swallow Hill. If she had five visitors a summer it was a big deal. And the guys she met waitressing at the ski resort up on Silver Mountain, well, even she wasn't that kind of desperate. Maybe if she worked her way up to Schweitzer or Sun Valley, but those were coveted spots on the ski patrol circuit and she'd bet the men-type opportunities weren't any more fruitful in those places even if by all rights they should be.

"But, Marta-*cara*, we worry about you soooo much!" Marta mimicked Mama's voice to a turkey vulture that carved the air at the first vista lookout, an hour up the trail.

Since when had her Mexican family become so Italian?

Again Uncle Manuel's fault. She'd been raised in a lingual hash of Mexican, Italian, and English. No wonder nobody understood her when she got angry—other than her own family, of course.

At the halfway point up the trail, she needed a break and dropped the heavy pack loaded with her next two weeks of supplies. She heard the bright *tink* and cursed. At the very bottom of her pack she'd tucked two jars of the spaghetti sauce that she and Mama had put up last fall. Still not really understanding Marta's isolation, Mama had insisted that Marta should have something homemade to serve if a nice man came by. The glass had broken against a rock when she'd unthinkingly dropped her pack. There was no point in digging the mess out now. She'd been right, glass was too heavy, but she'd been in such a hurry to get out of the house that she hadn't taken the time to empty the jars into baggies.

By the time she reached the summit, she had chaffed shoulders, a sore back, and the bottom corner of her pack and the right hip of her shorts were both stained tomato red.

3

————————————

etrick met her at the bottom of the lookout stairs with his pack already on. He headed down the mountain with barely a, "No fires. See you in twelve days." He was hustling down to be with his new girlfriend, whom she wished luck. Dating a lookout substitute meant that you saw him only briefly every three days, because the rest of the summer he was cycling up and down to various towers.

He wasn't her type anyway. He reminded her of all of the jocks who used to try and grope her in school. He seemed nice enough in the moments they traded places, and didn't stare at her chest—too much. He also left the cab as neat as he found it, which she appreciated but he never slowed down enough for her to thank him.

She did her first scan to confirm Detrick's assessment and then unloaded her pack. At least only one jar was broken.

Then she felt an itch.

It was the itch that her Uncle Manuel had tried to teach

her, "It is when what is missing is too subtle. You can no longer taste that you need more thyme or oregano, but you know that the balance, it isn't right. Then you must become very careful. A mistake now and the whole sauce must go down the drain. But still the sauce is incomplete and must be finished. Slow down and listen. You will feel an itch, a tiny push from some part of you that knows about food and flavors. What it tells you, that will be the right answer."

She felt one of those.

Marta slowed down, waited, putting everything away. Produce in the cooler, dry goods and cans on the shelves. Two new books, one only a little stained with red sauce, on the tiny shelf above her desk.

Out of the soggy shorts and into clean ones.

Then, rather than standing at the Osborne Fire Finder, she stepped out onto the narrow porch with her binoculars. She started the circuit at Gray Wolf Summit to the northeast because it was one of the clearest landmarks in the area. From the burn at the base of the summit, she swept slow arcs; first along the horizon, then lower and lower until she was looking down the cliff of Swallow Hill's north and east face.

Then she moved to the north side of the tower and did the same thing. She always went around it "contrariwise." Her dad said that she did everything backwards because she was left-handed. What had been an idle joke had turned into an act of defiance and finally a force of habit. She'd learned that doing things "contrariwise" let her see things that she wouldn't otherwise if she was being "normal."

She was around to the south side of Swallow Hill when she spotted the faint puff of smoke. It disappeared almost the instant that she saw it, because young fires could do that.

She didn't move the binoculars from that point for three long minutes.

The breeze was a light brush out of the south as well. And it carried…wood smoke.

Another puff and she had it pinpointed. Not taking her eyes off the spot, she fumbled around until she found the doorway into the cab. She spun the Osborne into position and looked through the two brass sights just as the smoke went from puffy white to steady gray.

She pulled the radio off her hip. "Gray Wolf, this is Swallow Hill. I need a cross approximately two miles south of my tower."

Tom up on Gray Wolf came back moments later, "Two-three-nine degrees."

"Roger that," Marta plotted the cross quickly, double-checked everything, then called Vic. "Fire control, this is Swallow Hill. Confirming new fire due south of my tower at…" she read out the longitude and latitude. "Just gone steady. No eyes on the blaze, but estimate one acre based on plume."

"Catching them earlier and earlier, Marta. You know this blaze puts you ahead of the all-time record: number of fires spotted by an individual this far through the season. Ten more and you'll break the all-time season record."

"Oh joy," she radioed back.

Vic's laugh made her feel worlds better. "I have a chopper heading your way. He's in the area, we'll get some eyes on the prize before we call the troops."

4

Marta ducked and cursed as the small helo buzzed her tower from behind. She'd been out on the south deck again, and hadn't heard him coming from the opposite side of the tower.

Helo 41 slewed to a halt, hovering, and turned so that the pilot was facing her from just a hundred feet away. The sun was behind him and she could only see the shadows of the man at the controls.

"Afternoon, Ms. Swallow Hill." Tyler. She did her best to avoid a girly sigh…and really wished she could see him better.

She pulled her radio off her belt and keyed the Transmit button. "Afternoon yourself, Master Tyler."

"I hear you found another one for us to play with."

She pointed down the slope toward the gray puff that was already going black with soot.

Helo 41 twisted to the left and she could see the silhouette of the pilot looking down and to the side, but still couldn't tell his age or build. "Yep, that does indeed look like you have a fire, Ms. Swallow Hill. And right on your front stoop."

Then the helicopter twisted back to face her rather than diving down for a closer look.

"If you don't mind my sayin', Ms. Swallow Hill. Never have seen you out of your glass tower before. I can see that I was missing a fine sight. A fine sight indeed."

Before she could think how to respond, he'd slammed over his controls and half rolled into a plummet down the valley.

So, he liked the way she looked. Big deal. Most guys liked how she looked. Then she raised her binoculars and focused them down the slope again.

"Wish't," she imitated his voice, "I'd a thought to look through this here contraption when you were a might closer, Mister Tyler." Instead of Tyler's smooth Colorado, it came out more Mexican-Italian-Texan which sounded even stupider out loud than she'd imagined. A burst of giggles tickled its way up her throat and she was never one to hold back a giggle when it came.

So, he thought she was pretty? Well, with that gorgeous voice of his, he didn't have to be a handsome one. Maybe she'd find a way to meet him…when there wasn't a fire on her mountain.

For now she'd just sit and watch the airshow.

5

---

*S*ix hours later she *wished* she could just sit and watch.

Tankers were on other fires. Helos were spread thin. Most of the smokies were in Colorado. And the Swallow Creek Fire was taking unfair advantage of their lack of attention. The south side of Swallow Hill was engulfed in flame and the plume of smoke kept blanking out Marta's view.

She'd retreated into the cab, closed the windows and doors, and donned a dust filter mask so that she didn't choke on the ash.

"Hang on, sweet thing," was all the warning she had before Tyler unleashed a hundred and forty gallons of water over her cab. It whumped down onto the roof with a crash like thunder. The half-ton of water striking in a single blow made the cab shake its head like a wet dog shedding bathwater. The structure shuddered and then calmed.

It was a good move, once she was over the shock of

it. Soak down the tower so that no stray ember alighted and caught the place on fire.

Soaking down the tower.

That was definitely not a good sign. You didn't do that unless the fire was close.

If she had to move, it was going to be fast. Her big pack would slow her down too much. She grabbed her fanny pack and shoved in a small medical kit along with spare batteries for her radio, and a water bottle. She pulled down her favorite family photo, parents and two hopelessly dense but terribly handsome older brothers gathered at Manuel and Graziella's wedding. She kissed the photo for good luck, snapped a can of bear-repellant pepper spray onto the belt along with a foil fire shelter— because a firefighter is always prepared, even when she's a lookout tower woman on the verge of totally freaking out.

And then she couldn't think what else to do.

The helos were losing the battle and she was losing options.

Ten minutes. She was a fast runner. Marta would give them ten more minutes and then she'd be jackrabbitting down the trail and to hell with the firefight.

6

———————

*a*t fifteen minutes, she'd eased down three of the five flights of steps, reluctant to leave the Swallow Hill Lookout un-womaned in the middle of a fire.

The air was thick with smoke and growing hotter by the minute. She could taste the char right through her filter mask. The fire's roar, always a distant thunder in her experience, was now a passing freight train. It wouldn't be long before it was a jet engine at max thrust, and just as hot.

At seventeen minutes, she'd made it down another flight and the steel handrail was warm against her palm.

Was the air clearer? Or was it her imagination? She looked up and couldn't see the cab at all. It was wrapped in a shroud of smoke that was climbing the hill and soaring aloft.

Okay. It was her imagination. That and she was getting closer to the ground.

The airshow had become a distant sound, muffled by the fire's thunder, but she could still pick them out.

Another helo had just arrived. A tanker as well. But Tyler had left to refuel just a moment ago.

She checked her watch, had to rub at her eyes to make them focus.

Duh!

Marta rinsed her eyes from the water bottle, dried them with the hem of her t-shirt, and then pulled on the goggles that habit had shoved onto her hair.

Now she could see her watch. Tyler had been gone twenty minutes. Long enough to refuel in Missoula and get back here? Probably. Maybe he was the returning helicopter she could hear circling above the tower. That meant there was still only him and the tanker. It made her feel safer, knowing he was close by.

She heard him setting up for another pass, then she heard a high buzzing sound—impossibly close to her. She thought she saw motion out of the corner of her eye, but it was gone into the smoke too fast to be sure.

Seconds later she heard an odd crunch. Something mechanical and it didn't sound good.

"Goddamn it!" Tyler. On the radio. Swearing.

That didn't sound good at all.

"Helo 41 report!" The Incident Air Commander called down when Tyler didn't continue.

"Hobbyist drone over the fire. It came up out of the smoke and I think I hit it."

"Any issue?"

"Assessing."

Marta tried to breathe. Tried to count seconds in her head. Tried to think of some way to help him—

"Mayday! Mayday! Mayday! This is Helo 41. Tail rotor not responding, I have to put it down, fast. Visibility zero. Mayday! Mayday! Mayday!"

"Tyler!" Marta screamed at the sky.

And then, almost as if he'd heard her, his helo plunged down out of the smoke so close by that it felt as if she could touch him.

A blade clipped the steel tower not five feet above her head. With a horrible metallic rending sound and a high whistle, a chunk of rotor blade flashed by her head.

She dove down the last flight of stairs, rolled on the ground, and looked up in time to see the helicopter hit the rocky slope, bounce upward, then thump down hard, crushing one of its long skids.

He'd been moving so fast; the helicopter careened and tumbled down the slope.

Marta was away from the platform and racing after the helo even while it still rolled. The five thin blades battered and flailed at the rock. Chunks flew in every direction.

A hard dodge to one side and a four-foot section missed her by mere inches. She barely noticed, her whole being focused on reaching Tyler through the mayhem.

The helo balanced upside down for a long moment, perched on the remains of its rotor head. Then in an almost lazy last gasp, it rolled back onto the meadow—most of the way onto its belly.

Marta reached the bird and finally realized where it had stopped. Another half roll and it would have tumbled right off of Swallow Hill, a two thousand foot fall down a cliff face too steep to walk without a rope.

She reached the door, yanking with sheer adrenaline until she had it free.

Someone was shouting on the radio.

Wasn't Tyler.

So didn't matter.

Tyler lay sideways in his harness. Slowly, so slowly, he twisted around to look at her.

He had a half dozen cuts on his face and was bleeding from several of them, but none of them badly. Despite the cuts and blood, she could see that while he wasn't beautiful—so much for girlish fantasies—his face had a ruggedness that was quite attractive.

He offered her a sideways smile, then hissed and reached up a hand to gently test a split lip. His eyes had not left her face for a second.

"Hello there, Ms. Swallow Hill. Sorry for dropping in unannounced like this. Poor form for a gentleman come calling."

"Terribly poor form," she did her best to match his tone. "Let's get y'all out of there before something worse happens."

"There's only one of me."

"What?" She climbed into the cockpit to help him.

"Y'all isn't singular, Ms. Hill. It's for a group of folks. Especially if they're from the Deep South, which I'm not."

"Then how's that sentence supposed to go?" She worked his harness free and did her best to ignore how close together they were in the tiny space, she kneeling on the tilted co-pilot's seat, him still strapped into the pilot's position.

"Should be: 'Let's get you out of there…'." He spoke in a deadpan accentless voice, clearly making fun of her, but trailed off in a way she didn't like.

There were no obvious signs of blood. So maybe he'd just been concussed rather than collapsing into shock. She'd taken the standard First Aid course for lookouts, but it wasn't much. The bottom line for a lookout was: do anything to yourself worse than a small cut and you're screwed. Help was a long way off.

Between them, they maneuvered him out of the cockpit. The smoke was getting thicker and she'd lost her mask and goggles somewhere during the sprint. A path of destruction had been flattened through the tall meadow grass by the helicopter's tumble. It was a wonder he was still alive.

"My ankle isn't working quite right."

They both looked down as he clung to her. It was twisted to the side. Grotesquely.

She looked at him, liking that he was a couple inches taller than her own height, and did her best to keep her voice light, "I don't think it's supposed to look like that."

"Not if I want to go walking anywhere on it," he agreed and continued to hang onto her.

"Where's my pilot? Tyler, report!" The ICA's voice screamed from her radio.

She pulled it out, "I've got him. But his ankle is broken. Request immediate medivac."

The stream of vitriol that poured out of the radio was quite impressive.

"You'll have to forgive him. He's rarely a passionate man, except about his pilots," Tyler whispered close to her jaw, with his nose practically buried in her ear. "Hey, Ms. Swallow. You smell right nice. Like—"

Something romantic?

"Like, tomato sauce."

Crap! She must have rubbed her hand in her hair while she was cleaning up her mess from the hike up. "It's an…old family recipe."

"Good enough to eat."

She considered taking offense, but if he was coming onto her, he wasn't doing it with a grope or a grab, so she'd tolerate it for the moment.

"Swallow Hill, this is ICA. I can't get to you. The entire peak is shrouded in smoke and you have my only helo in the area. Can you confirm the hobbyist drone?"

Tyler pointed with the hand that wasn't around her shoulder at the mangled tail of his wrecked aircraft. There was the remains of something white and mechanical caught in the rear rotor blade. She didn't know how to fly, but she knew a helicopter didn't do so well without its rear rotor.

"Roger that, ICA. Have visual on a hobbyist drone, or at least the remains of one."

"I'm gonna kill the bugger that flew that thing. I swear I am. Tyler, I have to pull back the tanker; I can't have him hitting a second drone. We can't get through the smoke even if I had a helo local. You'll have to take care of yourself."

Marta held the mike up to Tyler's mouth and hit the Transmit key for him.

"Not a problem, Mark. I'm right comfortable where I'm standing." And Marta was too. Very comfortable. He had an arm around her shoulders, and she around his waist, as if it was the most natural thing in the world for them to stand that way. He was just an inch or so taller than she was and she was upgrading that ruggedness to very good-looking.

"No," the ICA called back. "You're not. The fire is going to crest the ridge in ten minutes and there isn't a thing we can do to stop it, even if there weren't any other drones in the air and I had the full fleet. Swallow Hill, you keep my pilot alive, god damn it."

Though there was nothing to see, Marta became aware of the sounds for the first time since the crash.

She heard the heavy roar of the BAe 146 jet climbing clear of the area. High above, she heard the strong buzz of the ICA's twin-engine airplane circling thousands of feet above the fire.

Close to hand, there was a deep, basso roar that shook the air. So loud now that it felt as if it was shaking the ground.

"A FEAR fire," Tyler whispered, and this time she didn't feel any tease close beside her ear.

It was the worst stage of a wildfire before it overran you, the Fuck Everything And Run moment.

7

"Ten minutes," Tyler sounded perfectly calm. Dangerously so.

Marta remembered a cross-country race. She and a top runner from Boise had been deep in the woods and way ahead of the pack. They'd run against each other before and Barb was a tough contender.

Then Barb had caught a foot on a high tree root and crashed to the ground. And she'd just sat there. Cheerful. Glad to chat and answer questions. But she hadn't had a single thought for the race. No complaints while Marta had checked both her ankles which appeared fine. Barb hadn't had any reaction even when she looked down at her broken wrist bent over backward. So decisive just a moment before, she appeared perfectly calm once injured.

Shock.

Tyler was in shock which meant it was up to her.

Hightailing it down the trail was no longer an option. She should have left twenty minutes ago; she checked her watch. Thirty minutes ago.

But at some moment very soon, Tyler was going to start feeling his broken ankle.

The cab wouldn't do them any good, even if they could get up to it. And the shattered helo was no option at all.

"Tyler," she cupped his chin and turned him to look at her. "Hang onto the helo, I have to check something out."

He grumbled about trading soft-and-warm for hard-and-metal, but made the shift.

Marta crawled back into the cockpit and looked around, but couldn't see it. It had to be here somewhere. She stuck her head back out.

"Where's your emergency shelter?" The foil shelters were the tool of last resort and she knew the pilots had to fly with one.

"In the door pocket, pilot's side," he said it with enough clarity that she wondered if he really was in shock, or if he was just keeping a humorous façade up against the pain.

She looked back down into the tiny cabin. There was no pilot's door, there was only granite and tufts of grass where it should be. Crawling back out of the cabin, she looked around, still no sign of it, though there was the debris trail that started near the tower and was scattered across a hundred yards of the slope, she didn't see anything as large as a door.

The debris field continued past the helicopter and…

She moved as close as she dared to the edge of the cliff and looked down through the thickening smoke. Fifty yards below them there might have been a piece of helicopter big enough to be a door, but it was far out of their reach.

She had the one shelter on her belt. But as tempting as the idea of sharing a fire shelter with Tyler might be, it wouldn't work. The shelter was designed to provide close protection for a single person. Maybe if they were both petite…but they weren't.

"Story of my life," she mumbled as she looked around the barren hilltop for other options.

8

*H*er final glimpse before shutting the lid was of thick black clouds of smoke colored with the deep orange of fast-approaching flame.

"And I had so hoped, Ms. Swallow Hill, that my first water adventure with you might include something like skinny dipping. Seems my imagining came close. Care to complete a man's wildest dreams, Ms. Hill?" She could hear his gentle smile even if she couldn't see it in the pitch black.

Marta appreciated it all the more because there hadn't been time to move Tyler gently. The sweat of pain poured off him, but he'd kept his tone light and friendly despite the anguish of getting him in here. Whether the effort or the terror had done it, he was shaking off the shock. At least for the moment.

They were submerged up to their necks in the concrete cistern of her lookout tower's drinking water. The heavy steel lid above them was closed, for whatever protection it might afford. Then, draped like an air bubble over their heads, she'd spread her fire shelter. It was the only chance they had. *Santa Maria Madre di Dios.* Childhood prayers weren't helping her much. She focused back on Tyler, except she couldn't see him in the dark.

"How about a rain check on the skinny dipping?" She barely managed the thought around her raw nerves. Now that she had done everything she could other than wait, the impact of their precarious position was striking home.

"Rain, might help some. Douse this fire down a bit," it helped that his tone had finally taken on an anxious note. His voice was becoming clearer, recovering from his shock. Sharing her fear with someone else made the situation a bit more bearable. A very tiny bit.

A silence formed between them but she wasn't feeling very comfortable in it. The cistern was seven feet deep and, thankfully, she'd used up the top two feet of it in her first two months here. Thankfully, they were both tall enough to stand in the five feet of water still remaining, rather than Tyler having to tread water with a broken ankle. It was also just four feet square so they were jostling and bumping underneath the water despite having their backs pressed against opposite sides.

The water was cool, without being cold. At least not at first. It was starting to chill her and she could feel the panic approaching and...

"Talk to me, please!" She begged before she went off the deep end. The fire's roar beyond their shelter blanket and the steel lid over the cistern was muted, but growing fast.

"Right, my apologies, ma'am," his tone which had thinned a little under the pain had shifted back to more solid. "I was just a bit perplexed is all. By our current situation. It's awkward to be bumping hips and, uh, other things with a beautiful woman under such circumstances."

"Which are?"

"Ms. Swallow Hill, I don't even know your name."

Before she could answer, he hurried on.

"But your voice, you could make a man die happy just to hear such a thing over his grave. So sure and confident and female. It's an amazing thing, I'm telling you. And then when I finally saw you," he let out a low whistle. Not a wolf whistle, but rather one of deep appreciation. "I didn't know anyone built women who looked like you. One who stood as tall and straight as a ballerina but shaped like a goddess."

"Huh!" She tried to pull herself together. She really did. It wasn't working. "That can't be."

"But it's truth."

"But it can't," and she felt about as naïve as a swallow first leaving its nest.

"Tell me why?"

"Because…" She didn't even know why. "Because —" she tried again with no more success, having to raise her voice as the fire's roar built. "Because I'm no more ballerina than goddess. I guess the confident part is right…maybe. It must be, because it pushes men away like mad." And he saw the dancer in her? She could still feel that deep inside, but no man had ever said such a thing to her.

"Then you have been—and please don't take this wrong, Ms. Swallow Hill—spending your time with a bunch of fools."

She reached out in the dark, lost for a moment in the disorienting darkness, and tentatively brushed a hand down his chest. It felt safe and right, huddled together in here as the fire burned toward them. She suppressed a shiver against the cool water.

"Living in my glass tower, can't say I've been spending time with much of anyone."

"I like the sound of that even better. Less competition for me. Not so long ago I swore I was going to get to know the lady of Swallow Hill before this summer was over."

Marta could feel the heat rising to her own face and was glad for the darkness. "I, uh, might have made a similar swear about this certain deep-voiced pilot I know." Which she couldn't believe she'd just admitted. "Say something else. Anything else."

"Well…" he tried to keep his tone light despite the tension she could feel where her hand still rested against his chest. A good man to have around in a bad situation. "The skinny dipping wasn't a completely idle suggestion. I have a pal with a big ranch down in Texas. Horse ranch. Do you ride?"

"Willing to learn," she didn't let loose the bubble of a laugh building in her throat for fear that it would emerge as a babble of panic instead.

"Some fine places there to take a lady," Tyler continued resting a hand over hers, "if she's of a mind. Fine places. Not another soul for miles in any direction."

"I might be open to that," Marta slapped her free hand over her mouth. "I can't believe I just said that." The heat flashed back into her cheeks.

Then her face kept heating.

And heating.

Their breathing air was—

"Okay, Swallow Hill. You listen close," Tyler's

smooth and calm disappeared and he started speaking quickly. Dead serious now. "It's going to get hot in here, unbearably hot. And then it will get hotter. You hold down the corners of the fire blanket, keep its edges under the water. I'll do the same with my end. You're going to want to rip off the blanket. Don't! Our lives may depend on that."

Marta ducked her face down into the cool water, which only made the air feel twice as hot when she surfaced. She reached around Tyler, grabbed one end of the foil fire shelter and held it firmly behind him under the water. He did the same behind her. They were embracing…to save their lives. *Don't get stupid, Marta!*

"It all depends," Tyler continued hurriedly, "how fast the concrete and the water heat up. But do not pull the blanket aside until I tell you. No matter what. Do you understand? Do you…"

She nodded, which was pointless in the dark. They were going to be boiled alive. But she couldn't speak.

The concrete wall she was leaning against was no longer cold, it was comfortably warm. She shifted away from the wall, the warmth was creepy, felt dangerous.

Bumped into Tyler, chest to chest, but there was nowhere to go.

"Kiss me."

"What?" She had to shout to be heard over the building roar.

"I want to have kissed you *before* we survive this."

She wished she could see his face, his eyes, how he was looking at her.

The wall behind her was definitely warm now.

But she hadn't needed to see him before this

moment. She heard his voice, just as she had all season; it became the center of her thoughts.

She leaned in and kissed him as the roar deafened her. She clung to him as long as she could, but she had to break apart to get air.

It was so hot.

She dragged in a breath.

The air was fire in her lungs.

"Scream!" He shouted at her. "It's okay!"

The wall behind her was now hot when she bumped it. The water was starting to warm up. She held onto Tyler. Held onto their fragile shelter where it had been pulled down behind him. The air inside the small bubble of the fire shelter inside the concrete cistern was so hot it scalded her lungs. It—

The scream that ripped from her chest was echoed by the scream from his as the fire rolled over them.

At some point Marta stopped screaming.

The pain had eased.

The agony of each breath.

She floated in the dark, wrapped tight around a man. Around Tyler. Her end of the foil shelter was still tight in her fists.

"Am I dead?" Then a horrible thought struck her and she gasped out, "Are you dead?"

His soft chuckle reassured her infinitely.

"Can we open the shelter yet?"

"Not yet," his voice was a whisper.

"But the fire's roar…" It was gone.

"The area around us is still too hot. Give it a few minutes. Besides…"

"Besides what?"

"I wouldn't mind kissing you *after* we survived this."

Marta decided she wouldn't mind either, not with a man who kissed as well as he did.

They only had a few moments, that she thoroughly appreciated, before the heavy pounding of an approaching helicopter sounded loud outside the cistern.

Tyler broke off the kiss, but didn't release his tight hold on her.

"That, Ms. Swallow Hill, is how we know it's cool enough to leave."

Together they pushed the blanket up against the heavy steel lid and levered it open. It dropped aside with a loud clang of steel on concrete.

They tossed the foil blanket over the hot concrete and she pulled herself up to sit on the broad rim, and then helped Tyler up to join her. He flinched when he banged his broken ankle against her, but remained stoic. A good man to have beside you…beside her. A Black Hawk was settling onto the flat spot just below the tower. Everywhere around them was black char. The fire had burned every living thing in its path. Even now, other helicopters and a pair of tankers were battling the flames farther down the slope.

The tower!

She looked up. It still stood. The soaking Tyler gave it right before he crashed had saved it. The swallows swooped in, complained that the box was gone, had been burned away, and then all flew off again.

"I'll bring you a new one next year," she called after them.

A silence settled as the Black Hawk's engines wound down.

"You're all red, Ms. Swallow Hill."

They only had moments before his friends arrived from the helicopter.

She was worried about facing Tyler. They had been

through the heart of a fire together. They didn't know each other—but they'd said things. Shared things.

Be brave! She forced herself to look at him.

"You too." Bright red. His skin flushed brighter than a sunburn though she could see it was easing already. "Cooked like lobsters."

"Could be our first dinner date," he noted in that dry tone of his.

"Not a chance. Never had lobster and now I never will." Then she thought that, of course, she should have known—her Mama was always right. She nodded up toward the tower, "But you come visiting and I'll make the best spaghetti sauce you've ever had."

His smile was deep and proved that rugged and handsome could definitely be on the same face.

"Tell me one thing, Ms. Hill."

Her courteous, deeply-voiced Coloradan was back. With his easy humor and very good face. A man she wouldn't mind getting to know much, much better.

What secrets could she keep from such a man?

Tell him one thing?

"Anything," and she knew it was a promise.

"What's your name, Ms. Swallow Hill?"

"I offer you 'anything,' and that's the best you've got?"

She tried to shove him back into the tank, but he caught her up in his arms and gave her one of those deep, desperate kisses. Just like when they'd been at death's door, except now he was just doing it because he wanted to.

Because she wanted him to.

SUMMER OF FIRE AND HEART

*Quite how **Ashley Mason** made the journey from rural Kansas to working atop a lookout tower in the Idaho wilderness eludes her. This summer's challenge: coping with isolation.*

*   **Brent Tucker** dedicates every summer to learning something new. In the past he pursued competitive swimming and ballroom dancing. This summer's goal: to master hang gliding.*

*   This year they both will learn more than they bargained for during the Summer of Fire and Heart.*

This story sprang up because Ashley had been such a joyous character when I first discovered her in a New Jersey cowboy boot shop.

No, really!

You don't believe me? Just thumb on back to Night Stalkers #7, *By Break of Day*. She sells a pair of cowboy boots to the heroine.

But it wasn't only her fun voice that I wanted to follow up on. I'm also constantly fascinated by how we touch and affect those around us. What is a simple, unheeded moment for us, could thoroughly alter someone else's life as Justin does for Ashley.

On top of that, doing something new—which is Ashley's break from her past—became the theme of the story. Perhaps even more than Ashley, the story is about the power of adventure.

I have done several out-of-the-box, non-"normal" things in my life and the payoffs have been extraordinary. That's not to say they weren't scary, but they were almost always worthwhile. I took off work for a summer to rebuild a fifty-foot sailboat (which ended up taking three years mixed in with another job), and it taught me how to really sail. Years later—as a cure for corporate burnout—I bicycled solo around the world for eighteen months. Ultimately, on my scariest and best adventure of all, I decided to leave the corporate world and become a full-time writer.

But the daily adventures have sometimes also had an amazing impact upon me. So this is a story about a woman who takes a big leap and a man who takes many smaller ones.

1

*A*shley Mason had gotten exactly what she asked for and was at a complete loss of what to do about it. The scenery from her fire lookout tower was incredible; the Bitterroot Wilderness stretched away in every direction. Rocky Mountains soared and steep-walled valleys plunged, all of it thick with pine trees of the darkest greens she'd ever seen.

Mount Sunflower—the highest point in her native Kansas at four thousand and thirty-nine feet, rising from the surrounding countryside by a whole nineteen feet—wasn't much higher than the valley floors here.

Her perch for the summer atop Medicine Point, which was the biggest mountain she'd ever been on, stood over two Kansases high with room to spare.

And she would kill for a latte right now. But the nearest refrigerator was a gazillion miles away, so no milk. She wasn't desperate enough to make one with non-dairy powdered creamer yet…but she was getting there.

The sky here was amazing, and she tugged down on

her Kansas City Royals baseball cap so that she didn't have to see so much of it. The blue sky above went on almost as forever far as the green below and it was unnerving her.

It was all that cowboy's fault. There she'd been, happy as a pig in a poke to be out of Kansas. Paramus, New Jersey wasn't exactly the center of the universe, but it was such a relief from the endless flat of Hepler—a town that only existed because some fool had run two roads together out there in the middle of corn-fed nowhere with no thought about the trouble that would be causing future generations like hers.

She'd been aiming for the Big Apple, but found an authentic Western wear boot shop in Paramus, New Jersey just before crossing the Hudson River and never quite finished the journey. It was just as well, her visits to the Big Apple almost convinced her that Hepler, Kansas wasn't so bad after all. But Ashley had dug in there just fine; not enough to plant roots, but just fine. She knew how to sell it with her Kansas accent, her track-and-field body, and her long blond hair. While there she'd accumulated a cheap apartment, an okay boyfriend, and a rattletrap Ford F150 that was now parked a three-hour hike down the mountain.

She'd been the queen of boot sales. No customer who came into the shop—especially not the really handsome ones—had managed to escape her clutches without a new pair of boots. It didn't matter how city they were; she could convince them that the only way to get a girl like her was with a fine pair of cowboy boots. Of course she never dated a customer, but she sure as shootin' knew how to sell them, each and every one.

Then that gorgeous cowboy had walked in, his

Amarillo accent ringing so clearly of the great outdoors that he'd ruined Paramus for her in the first thirty seconds. Worse, he'd had a Brooklyn girlfriend with him and bought her a three thousand dollar pair of Lucchese hand-sewn boots. Ashley had always lusted after a pair of her own but even the employee discount didn't put them in range. And she knew that if the cards were flipped, she wouldn't want to end up with some hotshot city boy after all. She wanted…

Well. That was the problem. She'd didn't know, but she knew she wasn't going to find it in Paramus any more than she had in Hepler. She'd wanted out and had grabbed onto the first thing that was the opposite of selling cowboy boots to city folk who would wear them to a bar one time and then stuff them back behind their Pradas, Jimmy Choos, and Fratellis.

And she'd gotten her wish—some fairy godmother really had it in for her—nothing could be more opposite to Paramus than Medicine Point fire lookout. Five months. She'd signed up for five freaking months atop the Montana Wilderness.

The first day she'd been gobsmacked by the wonder of it all. Days two through four had been setting up a routine and listening to her playlist—loud enough to drive out the silence…mostly.

Now it was day five and she was ready to bungee jump off her tower to end it all. The "cab"—her home for the next five months—was no bigger than a corn crib. The fourteen-by-fourteen foot box stood on stork-long legs of massive logs, twenty feet above the peak of Medicine Point. The summit was a craggy field with a couple of small campsites nearby, and then dramatic vertical plunges in every direction except the knife-edge trail that led back toward her truck.

Her nearest neighbor wasn't much closer than the nearest latte. Cougar Peak, The Lonesome Bachelor, and Old Crag lookouts were perched atop neighboring mountains, which meant they were twenty to sixty miles away. She could barely make out the towers through her big binoculars, never mind any people.

She stood on the narrow wrap-around catwalk, like a tiny summer veranda with a high porch rail. She leaned on it and looked down at the impossibly deep valley to the east. Any neighbor down there might as well be as far off as Paramus, except for her two days off every other week.

And it wouldn't do her any good even if she did come down off the mountain. The only towns within a hundred miles were no bigger than Hepler.

"Who knew that heaven would turn out to be such hell?" She asked the view. Gripping the catwalk rail until her knuckles went white, she screamed in frustration… and there was no one for miles around to hear her.

2

*B*rent Tucker nearly jumped out of his shoes at the scream that sounded just above his head. He'd thought he was all alone atop Medicine Point. Of course after the brutal hike up to the peak he hadn't exactly been focusing well.

He dumped his bundled-up hang glider—which had felt light enough five hours and three thousand feet ago—and looked upward. He'd walked right up beside the lookout tower to stare down off the rocky cliff edge at the jump he'd trudged so far to take.

Now he tipped his head back to look up and saw someone standing on the cab's perimeter walkway with their head down buried against their arms on the rail. All he could really see of them was a royal blue baseball hat with the letters KC on the front in white.

"You okay?"

With a squeak of surprise the person raised their head and looked down at him. Even the shading of the hat couldn't hide the piercing blue eyes that inspected him in some alarm. Then her—definitely a her, a pretty enough her to tie his tongue in knots—long blond hair fell forward and hid her face.

"Who are *you?*" She didn't even try to wrestle the hair aside, so he guessed that she could see him even if he could no longer see her. He had traveled around the country enough to know that her accent wasn't Texas or Oklahoma. It was Kansas…but it wasn't. Somehow it sounded softer and smoother than any of them despite the flare of anger behind the question.

"Brent," as if that explained anything. "Tucker," which explained even less. "Brent Tucker," he tried again, but talking to pretty women had always flummoxed him.

"Hi there, Brent." The "Hi" came out in a delicious cross of "Ha" and "Hey" and invited him to say something.

"Sorry to disturb you." *Sad, Brent. Real sad.* "I'll just set up and get out of your way. Shouldn't take more than thirty minutes."

"Thirty minutes?" She said it with a squeak of surprise and checked her watch. "Darn it!" And she disappeared from the rail.

He could hear her footfalls across the deck above him, but they stopped after a few moments, ending long before she could have reached the stairs down from her aerie. At a loss for what else to do, he began unbundling his hang glider. The faster he set up, the faster he'd be gone.

Once he had it out of the bag, he began piecing together the metal tubes for the wing edges and then the struts for the control bar. He had the wing fabric stretched and was just attaching the harness when a voice sounded close behind him.

"Sorry. I'm supposed to check for fire every half hour and I kinda forgot."

He spun to face her. Close up she had many amazing attributes. Tall enough to look him right in the eye, and a body in tight t-shirt and shorts proportioned to splendidly go with her height. Well-worn calf-high cowboy boots emphasized her long, muscular legs. Her blond hair was now back off her face, tucked through the rear hole in the ball cap. As pretty as she was, it was her eyes that commanded all attention. They were the same knockout blue as the Montana summer sky.

"What's that?" She moved to inspect his craft.

"A hang glider. Where have you lived that you don't know that?" *Continuing as smooth as ever, Brent.*

"Places where a molehill *is* a mountain. This—" she waved a hand at the vista, "I've never seen a thing like all this before jus' last week. Don't know as I ever want to again."

"Are you kidding me? This is glorious. I could look at this every day. This is one of the most unspoiled expanses of the forty-eight states. Every time I look at this I feel infinitely small and infinitely lucky. How can you not just love this?" *Now you're going out of your way to insult someone you don't even know. He should smack himself— would if he could figure out how to do it without looking even stupider.*

"I was already feelin' kinda small, and can't say as I'm much liking the help from the landscape." She turned from him to squint out at the horizon. "It's like it has secrets and no way does it plan on telling any of them, at least not to this girl."

"I'd think anyone would want to tell you their secrets."

Now she aimed that squint of inspection at him. He'd never flirted with a girl. He'd watched plenty of others do it, but his few attempts were always dismal failures. And now he was continuing his unblemished record of being an idiot around women.

His brain functioned on a perfect inverse proportional curve; the more attractive the woman, the more of a stumblebum he became. He'd managed to get up to the middle ground okay, where he could date a woman who was nice and fun to be with. But this Amazonian blond fire lookout was in an entirely different category and he was knocked right back into hopeless science geek.

To distract himself, he finished the inspection of his glider. Brent had planned to spend some time enjoying the view and he'd expected to spend a *lot* of time working up his nerve before jumping. He'd had plenty of lessons on smaller terrain, but this was to be his first major solo flight.

Under the fire lookout's watchful eye, he chose to simply strap in and get out before his congenital idiocy got the better of him. Someday he'd have to get over his awkwardness around attractive women, but this summer he had dedicated to mastering hang gliding. Maybe next summer he'd dedicate to learning how to speak to women…or studying to be a mime!

Without looking back, he clipped in, tipped up the wing, and ran for the cliff edge. Just as he launched into space, she called after him.

"My name is Ashley."

"Brent. Brent Tucker," he shouted back, which he'd already told her. By the time he'd thought to say more, he'd nosedived off the edge, rapidly gaining enough speed to properly fly and she was long out of earshot. The nylon wing snapped brightly in the wind as it filled and took shape. The wind was loud without roaring.

He had flown well away from Medicine Point before he thought to look back. He could still see the tall woman with the wind-blown flag of sunshine hair despite the distance.

With a banked turn he lost sight of her.

It didn't matter. He wouldn't be seeing her again. He'd climb some other peak for his next flight.

Then it struck him with surprise, he was flying clean without all the nerves that had plagued his last two sleepless nights and the whole climb up the mountain. He banked again to follow the line of Warm Springs Creek ever so far below.

Though he wouldn't mind if he did see her again… maybe next time he'd pre-plan a few sentences so that he could at least pretend they were having an actual conversation.

3

$\mathcal{A}$shley couldn't help giggling a little to herself as "Brent, Brent Tucker" had flown away. It had been a long time since she'd struck a man speechless. It was a nice compliment, and a surprising touch of reality here in the vast wilderness. Maybe she could do this.

She watched the bright blue-and-black wing dip and soar against the background of pine green and rock as he swooped along. Even after he was out of sight she watched the wilderness, wondering what it would be like to feel so free.

Hepler and Paramus had been so crowded. The former with all of her high school classmates who had just assumed that she'd settle down with one of them to be a farmer's wife. And the latter with so many Yankees that even the sound of her own thoughts had seemed those of a foreigner from a strange land—she'd kept adding more and more Texas to her accent just so that she still sounded like herself.

For an entire summer she would be utterly free. Able

to think and do what she wanted. Well, except for every half hour. She glanced at her watch.

"Darn it!" Ashley raced back up the tower stairs, ten minutes late for her survey for forest fires.

4

It had been a week since Brent had flown away from Medicine Point vowing never to return. And his vow was still firmly in place, even as he hiked the last stretch up to the summit for his second time. But in the week since, he'd obtained his H3 intermediate license and traded up his floater wing to an intermediate rig. It had a narrower but longer wing and he couldn't wait to test the performance off a big hill instead of a small training slope. And his best flight yet had been off Medicine Point.

Of course, the intermediate wing weighed another fifteen pounds more than the novice rig. Every step up the trail he'd cursed not choosing paragliding. The oversized parachute weighed under forty pounds, not over seventy, but he liked the feel of flying like a plane. Too late to switch, he'd already taken three weeks of lessons and summers didn't last forever no matter how much one wished them to.

As he approached the summit his steps slowed to even more of a crawl than they had while trudging up the long grade. The cab came into view and he could see her there behind the cab's big windows. She, Ashley, had her binoculars raised and was looking off into the distance.

The day was silent. A small flock of sparrows fluttered by in a quick twitter and a swallow soared about on the soft breeze in loops and swirls like a painter attempting to color the sky.

Ashley moved quickly and he could hear her voice clearly. She was practically shouting, "This is Medicine Point lookout. I have a smoke at six-three degrees. I think it's on the face of West Goat Hill."

A smoke? A fire? He scanned the horizon quickly but didn't see any flames approaching.

"This is Cougar Peak," another woman's voice crackled over the radio. "I confirm. One-two-zero for the cross, definitely West Goat. Strong white already going ash gray. Growing fast. Command, you'll want to get a team in there. Credit for sighting to Medicine Point. That's the first one of the season; I guess we all owe you a round when we get down in the fall. Your first fire makes you an official member of the club. Well done, Medicine Point."

"Thanks. That means I get to name it. Right?"

"You do. But we already had a West Goat Fire a couple years back."

Brent had eased his load to the ground and decided to brave the lookout tower to see the fire, and drag Ashley to safety if necessary. He was halfway up the steps when he heard Ashley's voice again.

"How about…" she trailed off.

Brent reached the cab's open door and raised a hand to knock, when she turned and spotted him.

"Flyer Tuck!" she exclaimed in surprise.

"Where in the world did you get that, Medicine Point?" The woman on the radio continued without waiting for an answer, "Okay, it's officially the Flyer Tuck Fire. Cougar Peak out."

Brent knew his jaw was down, but there was nothing he could do about it.

Ashley looked from him, down to the radio in her hand, and back at him.

"W'all howdy, Flyer Tucker. It seems you've gone and gotten famous. My first one! You're on fire, boy. Better yet, you *are* a fire." Her laugh was high and wholehearted, impossible to resist.

Brent couldn't help himself and joined in.

Ashley set down the radio, crossed the cab in three steps, then she threw her arms around his neck and kissed him. She'd clearly meant it to be a quick, smacking kiss. The joy was just vibrating off her.

To keep himself steady—actually to keep her impact from driving him backward out the door and head over heels down the steep steps—he grabbed onto her waist. Somehow that quick smack of lips turned into an embrace and kiss that quickly dusted his prior experiences. Kissing Ashley was a more energized and exciting experience than full-on hot-and-sweaty sex with anyone in his past.

"Wanna see?" She pulled back from his arms as if nothing had just rocked his world and, taking his hand, dragged him to the huge windows that surrounded the small room.

It was an efficient space. There was a cot and a cooler beneath a cook stove. A line of counters down ran one wall and turned into a desk by the door, a tiny bookcase was crammed with novels. Squeezed in by the foot of the cot were two small armchairs. One of those big circular fire spotter tools took up the center of the cab—he paused long enough to spot a label, Osborne Fire Finder, before Ashley dragged him the rest of the way to the window. The cab was small enough that there was only a narrow walkway between the device and the furniture lined up along the walls.

"There!"

Brent followed the direction she was pointing, but he wasn't sure what he was looking for.

"Here!" She shoved a pair of binoculars into his hands with the same enthusiasm she had kissed him. Then she guided him until he saw it: a small column of smoke climbing up and dissipating quickly.

"Not much of a fire." He didn't know whether or not he should feel hurt that something so small had been named after him.

"That's," she turned toward the Osborne Fire Finder, whirling quickly enough that he was briefly lost in a cloud of blond hair, "eleven miles away. I bet it's a couple of acres already. Sit. Sit. I can't wait to see my first air show."

"Air show?"

"Shh," she kicked a pair of stools out from under the counter. She perched on one and, taking his hand once again, pulled him onto the other stool to sit beside her. Neither did she release his hand, instead keeping it trapped between both of hers.

He looked at the sun. It was still early in the afternoon. He could wait a while, he'd just have a shorter flight than he'd planned. Besides, he liked the way it felt…as if they were already friends. As if they'd known each other a long time.

"What's an air show?" He whispered his question because suddenly the cab felt a little like a holy shrine. She was so intent that she created an immense stillness in the space.

She just shook her head, unleashing a shower of hair about her face and shoulders.

5

"There," Ashley saw it and pointed, causing their shoulders to bump together as they sat side by side.

"All I see is a big bird that…" Brent's voice trailed off.

He had a nice voice once he used it. He was a funny mixture. She'd always gone for tall and big shoulders. He was neither, but it looked good on him. His dark brown hair was long enough to make a girl want to run her fingers through it and the close-trimmed beard gave him solid, reliable look that she rather liked. Brent matched her five-ten and was just a normal-looking guy —strong but no football star.

As they sat here, she'd finally figured out that he was embarrassed to be around her. On his first visit, she'd been so frantically glad to see another face that she'd been a little ridiculous, nothing new for her. He'd certainly flown the coop fast enough. It was one of the reasons she was keeping his hand pinned between hers at the moment—she didn't want him flying away again so quickly.

"…that's no bird." He reached for the binoculars, but she didn't let go of his hand so he had to fumble for them. With her free hand, she pulled out a second, smaller pair for herself.

She also didn't want to let go because she was *so* glad to see another human being. If her first five days had made her crazy, an additional week atop Medicine Point had nearly tipped her into the deep end. Except the last day or so she'd started enjoying it more, going for a trail run before watch duty, and the dinnertime sunsets were spectacular.

But the real reason she was holding on was that she was having trouble breathing and was half afraid she'd hyperventilate and faint if she did let go.

It was crazy.

All she knew about him was his name, that he had a hang glider, and that he kissed like they did in the movies. Star-spangled fireworks only happened on the big screen, but having an airshow for follow-up was pretty darned impressive in her cowgirl's experience and his kiss had earned every diving run of it.

First a small plane flew in and circled high above the fire, little more than a black dot in the blue sky. Ten minutes later a big plane roared by close overhead Medicine Point, making both her and Brent duck and laugh a little nervously. It dove down into the valley and then climbed across the face of West Goat Mountain. It dumped a long shower of water and turned back to race away over their heads again, returning to base for another load.

They had to wait twenty minutes before the next event, then the air was suddenly cluttered with aircraft.

First, the huge tanker aircraft returned to dump another load, bright red retardant this time. Next, a smaller plane, painted black with red-and-gold flames down the side, flew overhead. In moments a half-dozen parachutes were floating down toward the fire. A pair of helicopters in the same paint scheme began flitting in and out over the fire dumping water or retardant as well.

"Look, you can see the flame now." It was both exciting and horrifying. She could easily cover the fire and most of the smoke with her thumb held out at arm's length. But there were trees burning and, more importantly, people down in that mess.

She barely remembered to check the rest of the horizon every thirty minutes—a pattern that was finally becoming a habit. The rest of the time she just sat close beside Brent.

They started talking about the fire and the air show; neither of them had ever seen anything like it. He was from Colorado, the eastern part, which wasn't all that much different from eastern Kansas. He'd graduated from the University of Montana.

"I'm not there yet," she told him. "I did night school online and have two years of credits." She'd never told that to anyone; it had always been her own private goal. "That was my ticket out of Paramus and a bonafide guarantee that I'd never go back to Hepler. With me gone, Hepler is down to a hundred and thirty-*one* people. The nearest high school was fifteen miles away. That's why I did so well at track-and-field. In addition to practice I rode my bicycle both ways to school because there was no late bus."

"We should go visit Lamar someday. It's huge!" Brent spread his arms wide, accidentally bumping her on the head. "At least by comparison. Seven thousand people. Impressed?"

"Terribly!" She clasped her hands to her chest as if about to swoon with delight. They no longer held hands, but still sat close enough that she could feel him there beside her. "What is a Colorado flatlander doing with a hang glider?"

The air show was fading along with the light. The fire was reported as contained and now just needed beating all the way down.

"I," Brent looked out the window, but she couldn't quite tell what he was looking at. "It'll sound stupid."

"I'm a Kansas farm girl who sold cowboy boots in Paramus, New Jersey. Top that one. I dare you."

6

*B*rent kept looking, but it wasn't dark enough yet. He couldn't see the reflection on the inside of the cab's glass—the reflection of a man he wouldn't recognize sitting next to…

He cleared his throat, still convinced that this wasn't really happening.

"I'm a first year professor at UM. They kept me on after my grad work; I teach undergraduate astronomy."

"Which has what to do with hang gliding?" Ashley's tone was light. She made it easy for him to talk and with the fading light he was slowly becoming less daunted by her beauty and more enamored of her innate warmth of heart.

"I…" *In for a penny, Tucker, in for a pound.* "My dad said I'd never amount to crap," he said it fast so that he wouldn't sound bitter. "Probably because he hadn't either. I decided that every summer—while school was out—I would learn something new, really learn it, to prove him wrong. I started a couple years back. I spent a summer learning to do long-distance bike riding, made it to Wisconsin and back. I worked a summer with a swim coach until I won a couple of amateur competitions. I did ballroom dancing last year. This year I decided to try hang gliding. I've got my H3—there's only one more level of licensing, but the H4 is a lot of work." Crap! This was making him sound like he had no direction at all. He loved teaching astronomy and working with the kids. It was—

"Ballroom dancing?" Ashley sounded aghast.

Perfect. She was one of those people who thought that meant he was some sort of pansy who—

"However did you talk to women who were your dance partners? I'm not sure how you're talking to me."

Not the response he'd been expecting.

Ashley kept proving that in addition to being beautiful woman, she was also a very insightful one.

"Um, I just focused on the dance. Started with a male teacher so that I could learn the woman's role and understand how I should be guiding her. Then all I talked about with any partner was the dance. And...I have no answer for your second question. You're just the type of woman who scares the crap out of me. Let's just call it temporary insanity."

She watched him closely for a long moment before speaking, long enough that he wondered if she'd ask him to leave.

"Show me."

"Show you what? Why I can't talk to you?" How was he supposed to do that when he was?

"No. Show me how to dance."

And, much to his surprise, he did. In slow, careful

steps, they worked a basic waltz step around and around the narrow space between counter and the Osborne Fire Finder. The sunset filled the cab's windows with gold, reds, and finally deep purples. When the only lights outside were a tiny spot of brightness from the distant fire and the rising moon, she lit a candle lantern. He could see their reflections inside the glass as they moved more and more in sync about the tiny space.

His awareness of her grew until it was more than an ache or a need. It grew until he was conscious of nothing else but the warmth and softness of her beneath his hands, of the wild, fresh smell of her, and of the musical ring of her soft voice as she took over counting the time and steps. They moved from the slow waltz to the Viennese. She flowed easily into the quick Irish and finally the almost slouching country-western waltz.

They staggered to a halt after the world outside had gone completely dark, and only the flickering candlelight coaxed the blue from her eyes.

How long they stood in the perfect frozen silence together, he didn't know. Then she stepped back out of his arms.

He had brought no sleeping bag or blanket, he'd expected to be back off the mountain still in the heat of the day. Where would he—

Brent's thoughts stumbled to a halt as Ashley reached down to her waist and then pulled off her t-shirt. Her bra was the same color as her eyes, and all he could do was stare in bewilderment as that too hit the floor.

When she stepped back into his arms, she moved all the way in. Her skin was a silken wonder and for just a moment as their lips first met, he looked at their reflection in surprise.

Then any thoughts other than the woman in his arms simply flew away into the night.

7

June slid into July then August. Ashley could only look out at the wilderness in wonder as each day dawned.

How had she ever felt alone in the Montana Wilderness?

Brent's schedule had slowly slipped around until he flew in the mornings and then hiked back up in the afternoon to lie in her arms. Sometimes they'd sit out on the catwalk for hours, staring up at the stars as he told her the stories of heroes and gods in the constellations. Other nights he'd tell her about spectral colors, fusion byproducts, and Doppler effects.

After feeling lost for so long—ever since the third day of her freshman year when she'd suddenly realized the small-town dead-end nature of Girard High School and Hepler, Kansas—she now felt as if the future was rushing toward her. She could practically hear it in the slow steadiness of Brent's breathing as he slept wrapped around her on the narrow cot. It was there in the sweetest of wake-up kisses, and in the little treats he would carry up the mountain with him for their meals—even one-cup cartons milk for her lattes, bless his soul.

On her alternate weekends down the mountain, he taught her to fly. She wasn't ready to tackle Medicine Point, but she'd flown beside Brent for three hours on an amazing updraft finally landing in the University of Montana track field.

She could feel him coming up the trail as she scanned the far hills to the south. Heard the slight clank as he dropped his packed glider at the foot of the tower and the vibrations as his feet climbed the wooden steps up to her.

He slipped up behind her, wrapped his arms around her waist, and held her close as she finished the slow turn and fire scan. He'd learned not to interrupt her or she'd lose her place in scanning the hills. The fire season had heated up and it was a rare day that someone didn't find a smoke. Her own count stood at twelve—in the upper third of the lookout pack, which didn't do her ego any harm.

But even his slightest touch left her needing all of her willpower to finish the job. When she did, and had turned and received a proper greeting, he pulled open his pack.

"Fresh bread. Aged cheese. Chocolate. Bubbly," he held up a bottle of sparkling cider. "I thought about bringing champagne, but I couldn't figure out how to keep it cold enough."

"What's the—" Then she stopped. She knew. Brent was such a romantic. It was three months today since he'd jumped off the cliff to get away from her. Of course he would celebrate their first meeting, even if it was an embarrassment to him, rather than their first dance or the first time they slept together. As she often told him, he really was too sweet for her own good.

She thanked him a little more thoroughly this time.

Then he held up a letter, "I checked your mail, like you asked."

8

Ashley's eyes went wide and then she looked aside and blushed.

Over the last three months Brent had learned a great deal about Ashley. And one of the things he'd learned was that she was almost impossible to embarrass. Her heart was so generous that it had let him in and there wasn't a sneaky bone in her body, but there was also a frank straightforwardness that didn't flinch aside from anything.

Yet here she was blushing bright red over a letter from his school. He'd wondered at it for the whole hike up. His summer was almost over. Hers would be too, whenever they closed the fire lookouts for the season, perhaps in another month.

He didn't know what he wanted to happen, but he couldn't imagine a life without her in it. They hadn't talked of the future, not a single word, too overwhelmed by how incredible the present felt. The return address on that slim envelope had suddenly dropped the future right into the center of his thoughts.

"It's…" she took it slowly from his nerveless fingers. "It's just this crazy idea I had. I didn't mean it to—" Then she tried again, but still wouldn't meet his eyes. "I just kind of hoped—"

Brent stopped her from wholly turning away by placing a hand on either shoulder. He tried not to hope that she'd done what he'd been praying for the entire hike up the mountain. He pulled out the pair of stools they had sat together on to watch the first of many firefighting air shows. He had to guide her onto one as he sat on the other.

"Just open it. Then we'll talk about what it means."

She nodded without looking up, her hair showering forward and hiding her face just as it had the first time he'd ever seen her. She fumbled at the envelope several times and then finally just shoved it into his hands.

Ashley didn't speak, didn't look up as he worked the seal.

Careful not to look at the contents, he tried to hand the open envelope back to her, but she refused.

He rested a hand on hers and it was shaking.

Unsure of what else to do, he pulled out the single sheet. He started reading it aloud.

"Congratulations," was as far as he got before she screamed just as loudly as that first time and then clapped both hands over her mouth

Now she looked up at him and he brushed back her hair so that he could see the most amazing eyes there ever were.

"I hoped," she mumbled. And now her eyes pleaded with him, awash with unfallen tears. "I hoped so hard."

He read on against the tightening in his own throat. "School of Physical Therapy and Rehab. Track and field scholarship. Late start authorized at end of fire lookout season." He couldn't believe it. She'd be at UM with him. Ashley Mason wanted to be—

"I won't take it if you don't want me there," she spoke in a rush. "I didn't want to presume. But the way we—" she tried to hang her head again, but he stopped her with a finger on her chin. "I wanted," she finally choked out as the first tears fell. "I so wanted."

Brent couldn't help smiling. He too had hoped so much. And then in a fashion that he'd barely managed believe, he had taken action himself.

"I have just two questions, Ashley Mason."

She nodded furiously and covered her eyes in alarm and then uncovered them again without speaking.

"I know that it's too soon, but I couldn't stand the thought of you not being in my life." He pulled the last thing from his pack, a small velvet ring box. He opened it to reveal the small sapphire. "It was the closest I could find to the incredible color of your eyes. I want to look at them every day for the rest of my life. Please say yes."

She looked from his eyes, down to the ring box, and back. She opened her mouth, but nothing came out. After her third attempt, she just nodded. He had to hold her hand steady so that he could slip the ring on it. It looked far better there than he'd imagined possible.

He had to duck to kiss her as she kept staring down at it.

When at last she looked up at him, he had to struggle to find his own voice.

"My second question, and this is the important one..."

A look of worry slipped into her eyes and she clamped down her grip on his hands.

"We both learned so much this summer," he rubbed a thumb over the ring on her finger. "How, my beloved Ashley, do you feel about learning river rafting next summer?"

Her laughter, as sparkling bright as the sky above the Montana Wilderness, told him that he'd learned how to do this exactly right.

TOGETHER ATOP SAPPHIRE LOOKOUT

*Just before **Danny Chay's** life runs completely down the drain, an old friend bails out his sorry self. Bails him off the street and onto the 3,000-mile long Continental Divide Trail. What's up with that?*

***Lexi Forrester** needs a change. A summer as a fire lookout lies blissfully far away from her law-office past where she'd nearly lost all sense of herself.*

Until they both discover new paths Together Atop Sapphire Lookout.

One of my very favorite characters is Kee Smith (now Stevenson). She slammed onto the scene in Night Stalkers #2 *I Own the Dawn* (a seriously good title for Kee as I could easily see her taking personal possession of the rising sun itself). She has returned many times, most notably in Night Stalkers #3 *Wait Until Dark* and Firehawks #1 *Pure Heat*. She is *always* a force to be reckoned with.

In this story, I knew that I wanted to write another Fire Lookout Tower story, but I didn't know much more than that.

The first intriguing thing I came up with was the discovery of the CDT, the Continental Divide Trail. I had a friend who hiked the Appalachian Trail as therapy to recover from a horrific car accident during college. We talked at length about hiking the Pacific Crest Trail together, but life interfered (he fell in love and married) before our plans progressed very far. Even though it was first hiked while I was in college, I somehow missed the creation of the CDT entirely.

It was while researching other Lookout Tower tales that I discovered the CDT went right through the middle of the region I'd set my towers in. It starts in the New Mexico desert close by the Mexican border and runs all of the way up to the Canadian border at Glacier National Park.

My next question was who was the least likely person to walk that trail.

When I was a kid, our area of New York State had an experimental program that was both well-intentioned and ended in dismal failure. They took inner New York City kids out to the "deep wilderness" for a week-long "growth experience." In the woods not twenty miles from IBM's main plants (where my dad worked), these kids landed…

And freaked!

They'd never seen a forest or been in a place where the only sounds were nature's. With no preparation, they really couldn't handle it. It took a whole series of pre-trainings and smaller excursions before the program could get off the ground and ultimately I don't think it ever really recovered from that initial disaster.

So, inner city kid. But what motivation could he have to walk the CDT?

Enter Kee, my elemental force. She'd come from the worst parts of East L.A. She reaches in and drops my hero at the foot of the trail. It's his last chance and they both know it.

But who does Danny meet? And how do I write a love story between two people separated by over three thousand miles of rugged countryside?

Well, that's the fun of this story.

1

anny Chay reached the fire lookout tower in the heart of the Sapphire Mountains and decided that this was about the most crazy-assed thing he'd ever done. Sapphire Mountains sounded like some kinda girly shit, at least until he'd hiked into them. The rugged rock peaks of southwestern Montana jagged upward out of forests so thick that there was no way to see the ground beneath them.

Four months ago he'd never seen more trees than a city park. And the parks in East LA weren't exactly about Mother Nature—more like a quick drug deal or a fast, cheap screw. Didn't matter what color you were, hanging with the bros was about the only other thing going down.

The view from standing beside Pintler fire lookout tower swept a vast circle in the heart of the Idaho and Montana wilderness. Ten-thousand-foot peaks and dark green forest ran as far as the eye could see in every direction. No hazed gray sky here; it was so blue that it hurt to look up.

He didn't know whether he hated the woman who'd sent him on this damned quest, or if he should kiss her feet. But Kee Stevenson was someone you sure as hell didn't argue with.

She'd rolled back into the neighborhood after most of ten years gone, driving an immaculate, late-model, black Chevy Suburban, kind the Feds drove—which had scared him crapless even though he'd been clean at the time.

The tinted driver's window had slid down and there was Kee.

"Chay."

"Smith. Thought you were dead."

"Stevenson now."

Good as dead. He'd never figured her for the settling down kind.

"You want your shot at getting a life? Get in."

Anyone less dangerous than Kee, he might have tried rolling her for the wheels. Fifty grand on the hoof, ten to fifteen at the chop shop. She was maybe half his size, but if it came down to taking bets in a scuffle, he'd put his money on her.

Danny looked at her, same as ever. Half Asian and half who-knew-'cause-Mama-sure-didn't as she called herself. Serious body totally built to last and the best shot with a handgun he'd ever seen.

He checked the area. No one in obvious sight, but he could feel folks scanning him.

Hey, check out Danny kissing up to the Feds. What's up with that shit?

He could talk that down…not a lot of people dared mess with him, even after Kee bugged out. But that was the point, she'd found a way out. They'd talked about it a lot back in the day. Never seemed possible. When she'd evaporated, he'd assumed the street had swallowed her up.

But Kee never spoke anything but the cold, hard truth. She'd found a way out and all these years later had come back to offer it to him.

He got in.

Straight through the night she'd driven in silence, but she'd always been that way, even back when they ran together on the streets. They'd been tight. Not that kind of tight, but the kind where you knew if she had your back there were no worries coming from that direction.

East. She drove way the hell east into the kind of land he'd never seen. Deserts drier than the LA streets during the Santa Ana winds. Places where the next building was fifty miles away.

She'd finally pulled over in nowhere New Mexico desert just after sunrise.

"Out. Your gear is in the back."

"What the f—" But he'd chopped it off when he'd seen her look.

He'd slouched around to the back of the Suburban, popped the rear door, and tried to make sense of what he was looking at. It was a pristine backpack. Not the school books kind for geeks, but one near as big as Kee. Straps sticking out of it in every direction, it was the craziest looking thing he'd ever seen.

She came around and dragged it out, like it was heavy. Held it up while he slid his arms into place, then she let go and he'd nearly hit the ground. It wasn't just heavy, it was like filled with a Chevy straight-six engine block. Before he could complain, she had him strapped in and cinched down.

He half expected her to padlock it on him, but she didn't.

Instead she'd handed him a book: *Hiking the Continental Divide Trail.*

"What the f—"

"You already said that. You're here," she flipped it open to a picture that looked just like the man-tall concrete monument standing twenty feet away in the blazing sun. It was weird, like he was actually in the book. "When you get to the other end," she flipped to the last page to show him, "there's a phone number of a good friend of mine at a place called Henderson's Ranch in Montana."

"This is my magical out? Walking to fucking Montana? Have you totally lost your shit, Kee?"

She'd slammed the back of the Suburban and headed for the driver's door, but stopped the moment before climbing back in.

"You want it, Danny? You've got to prove just how bad you want it. Don't disappoint me." Then she'd slammed the door and was gone in a cloud of dust.

No one had ever believed in him. No one but Kee. He could argue with anything but that last line.

He had staggered up to the trail's entrance sign. It said that the spot was named for a crazy cook who had committed cold-blooded murder on this spot in 1907. He was totally down with that.

A cardboard sign flapping in the dusty breeze read, "Canada, 3,100 miles. Pure Hell, 100 feet."

No shit.

2

---

*L*exi Forrester decided to live up to her name.

"I'm so done with this," she'd told her business partners.

"You don't walk away from a successful law firm just two years after making partner."

"Watch me!" She'd dumped her caseload right there on the conference room table. No longer her problem. How many more times could she stand to face: "My parents never wrote a will." Or "I want to sue that cheater until he roasts in hell." Or "I was under mental duress when I pulled that knife in a bar brawl." Or…

Or nothing. She was done. Law school. The bar. Seven years climbing up the partner track and making it—

She was so done.

If she never saw Boise, Idaho again it would be too soon.

Her best friend, her mom, and her judicial-clerk-sometimes-boyfriend had all protested that she was having a nervous breakdown. Dad was the only one who offered any encouragement, a "just maybe" tilt of his head and shrug while Mom had ranted—or maybe he'd just been cracking his neck. It was always hard to tell with him. She'd been half afraid Mom would have her committed before she could escape.

Lexi had chosen something completely different from anything she'd ever done before. From anyone she'd ever *been* before. It was just one summer, but it was would make a clean break.

She hoped that spending a season working as a fire lookout high in the Sapphire Mountains would let her see what she was going to do next. So far, she wasn't having much luck with that.

3

---

*I*t *had* been hell. Danny had never appreciated the luxury of a water faucet as much as he had tromping through the New Mexico desert.

He'd quit a hundred nights on the trail, but woken up in the morning and forced himself back into motion. Sometimes it was imagining what the homies would be thinking if they could see him, grunting out another day —not a one of them lame-asses could do this kinda shit. It took digging deep and those squatters didn't know dingo-crap about that. Neither had he, but he was learning.

Sometimes it was the thought of Kee kicking his ass if he quit.

No, that wasn't her style. If he quit, she'd leave him in his gutter to die. Which only made him dig in harder.

Eventually though, once he'd gotten over the misery of the daily grind, he'd gotten to noticing the countryside around him. The desert wasn't barren. "Cactus is what grows in the desert," is what he would have said if you'd asked him before. But so did twisted pine trees that offered welcome shade. He saw hares, deer, coyotes, and more types of birds than he'd known existed. At one of the little towns he'd considered grabbing a book about them, but it weighed too much. He might have gotten used to hauling around a Chevy straight-six engine block on his back, but he didn't want to upgrade it to a Ford V-8.

Decent boots were swapped for good ones…he'd found an envelope for expenses stuffed deep in the pack. Along with a list of mail drops. At each drop there'd been a case of food, some emergency shit for blisters and such that he appreciated, and just enough cash to either see him home or on to the next mail drop.

Not a single word from her. He'd known she was a tough bitch—had to be to survive the kind of shit she'd been through even before she bugged out. But he had no idea how tough until he began climbing toward the San Juan Mountains.

There were route choices along the way. By the time he hit the first big one in Colorado, there was no way he was taking the easy path. Screw the Creede cut-off, he punched right up above the tree line—half the nights waking up to find frost on his bag, tromping through late snow during the day.

Nothing had prepared him for the plains of central Wyoming, the crazy steep Tetons, or the wonders of Yellowstone.

A lot of alone time out on the trail. Vast amounts of it. He'd hiked for a week with a very giving and seriously well-built woman named Crissy through a section of Colorado. He'd promised to stay in touch though they both knew he never would. But he'd seen less people in three months than he'd see in a typical LA afternoon.

Somehow, the whole thing caught up with him as he climbed up the trail to Pintler fire lookout in the southwest corner of Montana—his last state, the brutal Idaho Bitterroots thankfully behind him.

4

Mid-summer was mostly gone from her eagle's aerie atop the Continental Divide, eight thousand feet up in the Sapphires. Lexi hadn't made any progress toward what came after the fire lookout job, but she wouldn't trade this summer in for the world.

She'd made radio friends with other lookouts and spotted her fair share of forest fires, but mostly, she'd had nothing but the wilderness and time.

Oh, she'd ridden through all of the ups and downs they'd warned her about. Horror at the choices she'd made in burning her bridges in the Boise legal community. Wondering if she'd lost her mind to make this crazy choice in the first place. Depression that she was having a mid-life crisis before her thirtieth birthday —she'd always been an overachiever, but this one she could have done without.

But she'd also slowly regained her equilibrium, something she'd lost a long time ago. She'd taken to rising with the sun and going for fast hikes and eventually mountain runs before her nine a.m. spotter duties began. She'd been track-and-field in high school, especially the shorter distances. The fast, brutal sprint—the high adrenaline of both the challenge and the victory—had fit her like a glove. Now she discovered the attraction of the longer runs, letting nature just sweep by as she ran through trees, past lakes, and over hills.

Lexi knew reality would come crashing back through her front gate in another couple months, but she was going to avoid it as long as she could.

On the radio she'd made the day's final "no smoke" call except for the fire still being fought on West Goat Mountain—one of hers. Chatted for a few minutes with Patty who said the wolf pack she was following had veered north, so no visit this time—bad news for Lexi and for Patty's husband up at Gray Wolf Summit lookout. Tess and Marta were trading recipes. Signing off, Lexi took a mug of tea and went to sit on her lookout tower's verandah to admire the sunset. Verandah, fancy word for the narrow wooden service walkway around the outside of the small cab that was her home.

The sky was just shifting from blue to gold when she heard the happy sigh of someone sloughing off their pack at the campsite below. She'd learned to recognize a lot by that sound. Pintler Lookout lay directly on the Continental Divide Trail, and its high peak always seemed to be the end of a hiker's day.

Some were short-section hikers, taking a week or two summer's vacation to do a stretch. Their groans were far more heartfelt, often accompanied by hisses of pain. But once settled, they were a generally cheery group, teasing each other good naturedly about their next vacation being in Hawaii.

In early summer, the ones hiking the trail from north to south—Canada to Mexico—had six hundred miles under their belts by the time they reached her. Grumbling and discouragement were common: not yet through the first of the five states on the route most found to be brutally depressing. She'd taken to avoiding them when she could, hiding two stories above in her tower. It was amazing how few of that type climbed the last sets of stairs to admire the view. The last of the "sobos," the south-bound through-hikers, had dwindled out by July. Any later and they'd get caught in the snowy peaks in Colorado.

This time the sigh was different and she leaned over the railing to see why.

5

"Pintler Lookout," Danny said it aloud to hear his own voice in the vast silence. The only other noises were the rustling of a soft breeze through the low grass and a bald eagle crying somewhere far above.

The silence, which had creeped the shit out of him even more than the scorpions and rattlesnakes those first few weeks, was now an easy place to be. Even the memory of East LA noise, the car horns, the sirens, the hard laughter…all of it made him wince.

Had that been Kee's plan? Ruin his past by giving him a new view? If so, it had sure as hell worked. He'd given up wondering about that phone number on the last page of the trail guide. Whatever the future held for him, didn't matter. For now he was down with the moment. Getting through each day. Seeing what it would bring. Wasn't a soul in his old neighborhood that had seen shit like this view or breathed air this clean.

He dumped his pack but stayed standing, shaking out the familiar buzz in his legs. That was another thing they'd never believe back home. Walking over two thousand miles, he was strong enough now to squish any ten of his pals. He'd had to buy new jeans and shirts twice on the trip because they'd gotten too tight.

"Hi," a voice floated to him through the still air.

For a second he thought he'd imagined it.

"Where you in from?"

He looked around, but he was the only one here. "Uh, New Mexico."

"My first nobo," the voice was soft, unaccented, female. Had he suddenly lost his mind? It was like the mountaintop was asking him questions. "Straight through?"

"Uh-huh. Twenty-three hundred miles or some such, so far."

"Ahead of the whole pack."

Danny hadn't known that, but liked it just fine. He'd dusted any number of folks on the trail, once he got his feet under him. Not a single north-bound through-hiker ahead of him. That explained why the trail had been so lonely. He'd camp with sobos for a night or north-bound section hikers for a couple days to a week, but mostly it had been him and the trail.

"By yourself?" This time he caught the direction of the voice and looked up. A face was peering down at him over the railing on the lookout tower. A bright smile and a mop of bright red hair turned dark copper by the golden light of the sky behind her.

"Solo," he confirmed. "You?" Then knew that wasn't the best question to ask a single woman in the wilderness.

"I'm manning the lookout this summer," a slight evasion, but not much.

"Nope," he sat down on his pack so that he'd look less threatening and turned back to the sunset.

"What do you mean, 'nope'?" The woman on high sounded confused.

"I figure you're womanning the lookout this summer."

That earned him a sparkling laugh that did funny things inside him. There was nothing fake about it. It wasn't the laugh of someone wanting something or cozying up to him trying to be casual, pretending that there wasn't about to be some kind of deal going down. It wasn't a laugh by some buddy because you'd cracked a dirty joke, no matter how lame, and the laugh was expected. Hers just spilled out into the sky.

Her light tread sounded across the platform over his head and down the stairs.

"Thanks," she said as she came to stand beside him. "I've been trying to figure out what I was doing here all summer. Now I know."

Danny scoffed, "Damn if that ain't a feeling I know. Don't suppose you can tell me what I'm doing on this hike? I'm doin' it, just still not sure why." Her silhouette was enough to tell him lean and fine. In jeans and a t-shirt she looked classy. Maybe the way she carried herself so straight.

"Nope," she admitted cheerfully. "Unless your 'manning' it."

Something about that was too accurate to keep inside and a laugh just burst out of him, echoing off the night.

Her bright laugh joined his deep one for a moment.

"You've got no idea, sister. Christ you have no idea." That's exactly what Kee had done to him—forced him to man up rather than slumming through life. It was like the core of the whole thing: this hike, his life. It was about time he took ownership of it.

"Danny Chay," he held out a hand. "From…shit, I don't even know anymore. From the Continental Divide Trail I guess." He sure couldn't see himself back in East LA.

6

"**L**canna Forrester, but everyone calls me Lexi." She took his hand and shook it. Normally she would have hesitated, especially with a guy who was so much bigger than she was. His hand completely enveloped hers. Normally she'd have had her can of bear-repelling mace in her other hand. But something about that contented sigh and his deep easy laugh had made her feel safe. No, it had made her feel welcome. Welcome on her own mountaintop, welcome in her own life.

"From," and then the joke slammed into her. She did her best to lower her voice and imitate his tone, "From…shit, I don't know anymore either. Top of the Sapphire Mountains I guess." Then the laugh burst out of her, bordering way to close to a choke.

"Better sit down before you fall down, woman." He moved over to a handy rock and waved for her to sit on his softer pack which was awfully decent of him. Her knees did give out a bit, dropping her down onto the pack.

"I think I just sat on your cooking pot," she shifted to a more comfortable position.

"Couldn't hurt the damned thing anyway."

His tone, his use of language—she'd only heard it in the movies, street punk grown man tall. A storm of nerves slammed into her and she clamped her arms together against the sudden chill. Should she get up? Would he let her?

But Danny did nothing but look back out at the evening. One she was sure that's all he was going to do, she did the same. Pintler was a promontory that fell away steeply to the east and west and was nearly a cliff to the south. The trail wound in from the northwest and departed to the northeast. The sunset turned the hundred peaks and the hundred thousand trees into a tapestry of gold-tinted pinnacles rising from the green-black hills and valleys far below. The last of the swallows still skittered across the sky, the bats weren't out yet.

"First star," he pointed west.

It took her a moment to spot it. "That's Venus."

"First planet," he said in exactly the same way, pointing again as if he'd just noticed it.

And once more she felt more desire to smile than to be afraid.

He was looking around the sky, apparently searching for the next one to reveal itself. It would be Jupiter to the southeast, but not for another ten or fifteen minutes.

"Are you a good man, Danny?" Now there was a dumb question. Like a bad one would tell the truth.

He glanced at her, then rubbed a hand across his chin. Clean-shaven, unlike most who hiked the trail. His hair was long, down to his collar, but had looked clean while she could still see it. It had looked nice on him, a little wild, a little dangerous, though not in a bad way. Not her type at all. In fact…

"A good man," he said it flat. "The way I'm guessing you mean it, sister, not very."

Her nerves slammed back in full force.

"But maybe," he turned back to searching the sky. "Just maybe, I'm starting to get there."

7

———————

Normally Danny slept the sleep of the trail hiker —lie down and crash hard. At least once he'd gotten over the vast silence of the night, and the startling tiny noises of different creatures. Lying beside the lookout tower, staring up at the underside of the decking, knowing that Lexi was sleeping right there, sleep had eluded him.

They'd talked a long time. More than he'd talked to anyone out on the trail, and about deeper shit than he'd talked about with anyone, maybe ever.

Not the past. That was so far away he barely remembered it anymore.

She hadn't either.

It was like they were both born at the start of this summer. He'd told her about Kee, but it was like his life had started the moment he climbed into that Suburban. Just "friend from my past came and hauled my ass to New Mexico." Nothing more.

They hadn't talked about the future either. Just the summer: his long hike, her long vigil.

When she'd finally stood, shivering with the chill night air, and wished him goodnight, she'd done one thing more.

She'd rested on of those fine hands upon his shoulder and kissed him atop the head.

"That thing about you becoming a good man, Danny? Sounds like you're already there." Then she'd been gone. At least from beside him, if not from his thoughts.

The next morning he woke to the sound of her tread descending the tower's wooden stairs. The unnaturalness of the sound dragged him up from his brief sleep.

She waved at him, then turned and ran off into the woods.

It was all he could do to wave back. He'd barely seen her the night before. Now in the bright light, he'd gotten an eyeful. She was tall, maybe most as tall as he was. Her brilliant red hair cascaded and curled down to her shoulders. Lexi was as fine as a willow branch…he knew what those looked like now. Her shorts revealed long runner's legs and her t-shirt revealed not one extra ounce anywhere.

He couldn't believe that she was alone in the woods. Why he'd smack her upside the head for being so damn stupid that…

Then he got to thinking about it, looking out at the vast wilderness. A woman, even one who looked that good, was probably far safer here than back in LA. She wouldn't last a minute on his streets. There was too much fresh air and innocence about her.

Innocence wasn't right either. She'd clearly seen

some shit. Not his kind of shit, but enough to make her pretty disappointed in the world.

But there was lightness about her. He could still hear her bright laugh. It had made him tell his hardest, blackest moments of the hike in such a way as to get her to let loose that laugh some more. And she'd done the same. He could feel her doing it, as they'd sat on pack and rock near enough to whisper, digging deep into the internal shitheap and reforging it in the night.

He'd planned to just overnight here. Thought about it some more. It might be best if he did go, maybe best for both of them. He'd just go up and check out the view from the tower, pack up, and get out. He unpacked the stove that had given him so much trouble at first, and started oatmeal in his bent cooking pot. Yanking and tugging on it didn't quite fix the damage done by Lexi's fine ass, but it was good enough for oatmeal.

More time with the leggy Lexi Forrester might give his needs a hard time, though he knew to keep his hands to himself until she offered. But he wasn't sure he wanted to break the shitbubble of his past and spill it out for her to see.

Four months ago, he'd been proud of that past. He had massive street cred. Not only was he a survivor, but he understood the power that came from protecting people, even from themselves. He was the one who talked them out of the stupidest plans, or at least tried to. He was the one who made a point of visiting his buddies in the slammer when they hadn't listened.

Talking to Lexi last night, going deep inside, he'd begun to understand how small his world had been. He'd become better than all that. It was the unknown future that was now scaring the crap out of him.

"You're thinking awfully hard there, Danny," Lexi gasped out from close beside him.

He looked up at her. Shaking out her arms and legs. Her chest heaving behind her thin t-shirt. Damn! He was as much of a breast man as the next guy, but who ever knew that compact could look so good. Forcing himself not to stare, he looked up at her workout-charged smile shining on her ever-so-white face. Freckles enough to be damned cute without enough to make her look childish. She was pure woman, and that was before he got to her dazzling blue eyes—darker, richer than should be possible.

"Thinking about the future shit I *don't* know," he managed. And thinking about the woman he'd like to.

"Don't go there."

He wondered which thought she was talking about.

"Every time I think about what happens at the end of fire season, it scares the pee out of me."

He was down with that.

"Bring your breakfast up when it's ready. I just need a minute for a washcloth shower and a change of clothes."

Now there was an image he was *totally* down with.

exi had her own oatmeal with raisins started before she felt the vibration of Danny's heavy tread climbing the tower. She waved him into the cab—the fourteen-foot-square room that was her home. It had a counter along two walls that was her work area, kitchen, and small library. Two chairs took another wall, and a cot and the door took the fourth. The center was dominated by the large circle of the Osborne fire finder—the lookout's main tool for mapping a fire's location once it had been spotted.

While she'd been waiting for him, she'd done another inspection of the surrounding hills, even though it wasn't time yet. The West Goat fire was smaller than it had been last night, the ground teams must have worked right around the clock. Nothing else new. It was either inspect the forest or go through some pointless straightening and cleaning routine for her visitor.

She turned to face him and took a step back into the Osborne. Lexi hadn't seen him standing up before. She was almost six foot, he had to duck to make sure he didn't bang his head on the door. So at least six three. And wide enough of shoulder that she was surprised he didn't have to turn sideways to step through. The cab suddenly felt tiny and claustrophobic despite the big windows that wrapped all the way around.

His heritage looked mixed, giving him darker skin than hers, which was true for everyone on the planet. But it was light enough that she could see the deep tan from his living outdoors for the last several months. Black hair, dark eyes, but he didn't feel dangerous.

"If I'm making you nervous…" he gestured toward the door with his bowl.

"No," she couldn't be nervous around him after last night's discussions. No one had ever spoken to her that way, laying out such deep truth. And, for the first time, it had made her do the same…something she definitely wasn't used to in herself. Even her internal dialog never did that. She'd simply been sick to death of lawyering and decided it was time for a change.

Danny really thought about things…about shit. She almost giggled at her own Dannyism.

"No, not nervous. At least not in a bad way," and she knew exactly what sleepless thoughts that had come from. "Just a little surprised at how big…" and there was no way to finish that sentence that would be in any manner seemly.

He waited a beat then filled the small cab with his deep, reverberating laugh. He made an Incredible Hulk-like motion, holding out his arms and pushing out his chest.

"You're going to spill your breakfast."

That deflated him as he re-angled his bowl in time to save his oatmeal.

She'd never met a man who laughed at himself so easily. Or who let her do the same.

anny was torn between which view to admire: the landscape or the woman. All morning, with an interruption every thirty minutes for her fire scan, they'd chatted. Not the heavy talk of last night, but easy chatter of the day. She talked about running. He about weight-lifting. High school came up, but they kept it about the people when it became obvious that the two schools were different beyond imagining.

She knew her parents; loved them despite their flaws.

He vaguely remembered his mom before she OD'd, and kept that to himself.

A spaghetti dinner, he donated the pasta and she the sauce, had been about movies. He'd read some books, but nothing like she did. She pulled a battered copy of *The Bourne Identity* off her little shelf and handed it to him.

"Already saw it," he tried to hand it back. He hadn't even known it was a book.

"Trust me," she pushed it back.

And he did.

Sunset after her last sign-off had been spent out on the narrow porch. No room for chairs, just enough to clean the windows…or sit with their backs against the cab and their feet dangling off the edge, out beneath the lowest rail.

They didn't go deep like they had last night, instead they went quiet.

After four months, most of it alone, Danny thought he knew all the forms of quiet. But sitting shoulder-to-shoulder with Lexi Forrester, their tea mugs long since set aside empty, was something new. There was a depth, a texture, a…

For the first time in his life, he wished he had better words to describe things. Though he'd wager that all of the words in the world wouldn't let him describe Lexi even half what she deserved.

When she rose silently to her feet, he figured it was time to go. But when they reached the small landing between the stairs and the cab's door, she took his hand and tugged him through the door.

He didn't ask, for fear that she'd change her mind if he did.

She didn't say a word. Not then. Not when he took her in the silent darkness, just glad that she had protection because his was some impossible distance away in the pack at the base of the tower. And not when finally spent, she lay down upon his chest and held him.

Sex with Colorado Crissy had always been fast and hard. Almost like an echo of the street in East LA.

Lexi was like the mountains: fresh, full of surprises, and taking the long slow climb up with all the ease of a sunny day's hike. No one had ever given to him that way, shown him what was possible.

He'd expected the morning to be shy and awkward, so he'd held her close through the night, figuring he'd have to leave soon after daybreak.

Instead she woke and ran a soft hand over his bare chest.

Her first words were, "Can you stay a while?"

Not yeah, but hell yeah.

10

"**You** have to go!" It was going to kill her if he did, but she knew it was true. Somehow the summer had moved along and not touched them.

Danny looked up at her like she was ripping out his guts. The dawn light was just bright enough that she could see the pain as he lay on their narrow cot—after all these weeks it wasn't hers anymore, it was theirs.

"You know I'm right. The last of the nobo hikers are already racing through; you've seen them hurrying to beat the weather. After walking way over two thousand miles, quitting now with just six hundred to go…you'll never forgive yourself."

"I leave you and I'll never forgive myself!" His snarl appeared to surprise him as much as it did her.

She laid her forehead against his chest, his wonderful chest, and hid there. For an entire glorious August, they had lived in their mountaintop idyll. They'd only come down off the mountain once, a long hike out and back to restock supplies, the substitute lookout coming up for two days for that purpose.

Lexi was so completely gone on him that she couldn't stand it. If the future didn't hold Danny Chay in it, she didn't know what she'd do. Would he fall into the arms of some other lookout-tower babe or some trail-bait? She couldn't imagine it. Didn't want to risk it. But still she knew…

Danny began cursing. A long, effusive string of bitter anger. She was going to miss that. She was going to miss him reading aloud to her every chance they had. She was going to miss the incredible sex and the gift of lying in his arms. She was…

Going to make herself stark raving mad.

"It's not like I'm going anywhere," she managed.

"Neither am I, god dammit!" But she could hear now that he understood he had to go while there was still time—before the winter snows closed the northern trail. He just wasn't ready to accept it yet.

"You'll finish the hike and then you'll come back to me," she did her best to say it so that they'd both believe it.

"Said I wasn't going," though it was hardly even a snarl.

Crap! She was even going to miss his moods.

"I never was real good about staying in touch with women."

That jolted her upright, "But you are this time or I'll kick your ass!"

"Like to see you try, Lexi." That smile that he brought out when he was teasing her shown in the early morning light.

She leaned back down and kissed him hard, running her hands over his body until he groaned with his need for her. If it was even half the need she had for him, he had to come back. He just had to.

Six weeks without a word.

Lexi cleaned the windows of the cab one last time before re-hanging the heavy wooden shutters. The fire season was over. The first flurries had already painted the peaks white and the Forest Service was calling all of the lookouts back down. She didn't know where to go or what to do. So she took it by the minute rather than the day, ignoring the tears that kept blurring her vision.

Her pack was full. No garbage left behind. She'd bagged the books she'd brought in Ziplocs so that they'd survive the winter for the next lookout. She took only the Bourne books because Danny had loved them so. She could even hear them now, read out in his deep warm voice.

Danny Chay and Jason Bourne, both men on a path to discovering their true identity. The irony of that only caught up with her now and it made her cry even more than she already was. He was out there somewhere doing just that…she was the one who was completely lost.

She padlocked the door and descended the stairs a final time. The Forest Service asked if she'd be back next summer. Unable to imagine how she could ever come back to all of these memories, she'd refused. Next summer was too far away to think about anyway.

Next season? Crap!

The next *hour* was almost too much.

She couldn't even look at the tower as she walked away from it.

For three hours she descended the trail, hiking down into misery.

When she reached her Subaru Forester—"Lexi and Subaru Forester," how sad was that as a life's statement—and circled to the rear to stow her pack, the sight that awaited her didn't make any sense. She dumped her pack on the ground.

A big pack was already leaning against the Subaru's rear bumper. A pack that she knew because it had sat in the corner of her tower cab for a month. More battered. Snow crampons and an ice axe tied onto it, but still the same pack.

She spun around desperately searching…and saw Danny sitting on a fallen tree close beside the forest road.

Lexi didn't walk, she flew. Her landing carried him backward right over the log and onto the forest floor covered in fall leaves and deep pine needles.

He held her tight while she wept anew. It was all she could do. Nothing had ever been so big in her life and she simply couldn't hold it inside.

"You made it!" The first words she was able to gasp out.

"Mexico to Canada." By his tone she could hear how doing that had changed him. Made him more complete.

No, it had shown him that he was as complete as she'd already known he was.

He climbed back up on the log and settled her in his lap but she couldn't stop her hands from running over him.

"You're here. You're really here."

"Surprised the shit out of me too," he teased. "But after that place called Pintler Lookout, I could only think about one thing." He kissed her nose and she just leaned into him.

He told her about the rest of the hike, running into the high snows, but buying the gear and going for it anyway. Then hitching a ride back across Montana, rushing to get to her before she came off the mountain.

"I wanted to meet you up above," he pointed at the trailhead to the lookout, "but the Ranger station said you were coming down today. Didn't want to somehow miss you in the woods. Longest damned wait of my life."

She nodded. It was all she had in her.

"I called that number in the back of the trail book."

They'd both puzzled at that final instruction from his enigmatic friend Kee

"Open invite for both of us if we want to see what the hell winter is like working on a Montana ranch."

Again she nodded, mute with the wonder of the word "we."

"One catch though."

She looked at him and waited. Instead of the teasing

smile, he looked nervous. Lexi didn't know of a whole lot of things that could make Danny Chay nervous. When he didn't speak, she slid out of his lap and onto the log to sit beside him though she kept a tight hold of one of his big hands in both of hers.

"Turns out there's a reason other than the incredible color of your eyes that these are called the Sapphire Mountains." Then he nodded down.

In his free hand was a small velvet box. In the center of it was a silver ring with a single, brilliant blue sapphire mounted on it.

"It's not much, but it's all I could scrape together. I wanted to get you—"

"Shut up, Danny."

He looked at her in hurt surprise.

"Just shut up. If you say one more thing about something so perfect, I'll kick your ass."

He grinned at that. "Like to see you try, Lexi."

"I absolutely will." The laughter built inside her. She didn't know whether to look at the amazing ring or the incredible man offering it to her. "But first—"

"But first?" He frowned at her, the worry back.

"First you better kneel down properly, propose, and then put that ring on my finger like a really good man should."

And he did just that. Her incredible man who had hiked to her out of the wilderness, knelt before her, and, at a complete loss for words, used his eyes to beg her to be his wife.

Unable to speak herself, she just nodded and held out her hand.

He slid it on her finger and like a miracle, the future

wasn't dark or scary. It was as bright as sunlight on a mountaintop.

When he finally stood once more before her, she noted that the log on which they'd been sitting was close behind his knees.

He reached for her.

She shoved hard against his chest and he toppled once more onto the soft leaf and pine.

He managed to snag her hand as he went down and she happily followed him all the way.

LAST WORDS

Unlike the Firehawks Hotshots (or the yet unconceived Oregon Firebirds), I didn't know that this was the last story in the series when I wrote it. Instead, I was left looking for the next story on and off over the next year and never finding it.

Now, in retrospect, I can understand part of why.

Lexi is one of those characters that has more than just a little bit of me in her. I once heard Norman Mailer give a talk and he said, "For any character to come to life, he must be at least five percent you." Over fifty-plus novels and sixty-plus short stories I've found that to be absolutely true.

Perhaps each series I write is me hunting for some part of myself and trying to understand it better.

Sheila, the final heroine of the Firehawks Hotshots, carried a lot of my fears. The last story of this Firehawks Lookouts series carried a lot of my hope. I was lucky enough to find true love (twenty-plus years of it as of this writing). But I had to pass through a break from "my chosen life's path" far harder and deeper than Lexi's before I even had a chance.

I think that in having told that story, I had told what I needed to of my fire lookouts.

Or, perhaps, it could be a much more mundane reason. As I continued to study the lookout towers, I learned that hardly any were still peopled by Forest Service professionals.

The perceived "romantic glory" of the remote fire lookout towers is fast fading away. Now, small aircraft patrols cover much of that wilderness. And those are themselves being replaced by satellite observations. It made me sad to learn this and perhaps it took a little of the heart out of writing more stories set up on the fiery peaks.

But I love this five-story slice of the fire tower lookout world and I will always think fondly of these characters. I also always try to live up to their hopes and dreams.

WILDFIRE AT DAWN

(EXCERPT)

*M*ount Hood Aviation's lead smokejumper Johnny Akbar Jepps rolled out of his lower bunk careful not to bang his head on the upper. Well, he tried to roll out, but every muscle fought him, making it more a crawl than a roll. He checked the clock on his phone. Late morning.

He'd slept twenty of the last twenty-four hours and his body felt as if he'd spent the entire time in one position. The coarse plank flooring had been worn smooth by thousands of feet hitting exactly this same spot year in and year out for decades. He managed to stand upright…then he felt it, his shoulders and legs screamed.

Oh, right.

The New Tillamook Burn. Just about the nastiest damn blaze he'd fought in a decade of jumping wildfires. Two hundred thousand acres—over three hundred square miles—of rugged Pacific Coast Range forest, poof! The worst forest fire in a decade for the Pacific Northwest, but they'd killed it off without a single fatality or losing a single town. There'd been a few bigger ones, out in the flatter eastern part of Oregon state. But that much area—mostly on terrain too steep to climb even when it wasn't on fire—had been a horror.

Akbar opened the blackout curtain and winced against the summer brightness of blue sky and towering trees that lined the firefighter's camp. Tim was gone from the upper bunk, without kicking Akbar on his way out. He must have been as hazed out as Akbar felt.

He did a couple of side stretches and could feel every single minute of the eight straight days on the wildfire to contain the bastard, then the excruciating nine days more to convince it that it was dead enough to hand off to a Type II incident mop-up crew. Not since his beginning days on a hotshot crew had he spent seventeen days on a single fire.

And in all that time nothing more than catnaps in the acrid safety of the "black"—the burned-over section of a fire, black with char and stark with no hint of green foliage. The mop-up crews would be out there for weeks before it was dead past restarting, but at least it was truly done in. That fire wasn't merely contained; they'd killed it bad.

Yesterday morning, after demobilizing, his team of smokies had pitched into their bunks. No wonder he was so damned sore. His stretches worked out the worst of the kinks but he still must be looking like an old man stumbling about.

He looked down at the sheets. Damn it. They'd been fresh before he went to the fire, now he'd have to wash them again. He'd been too exhausted to shower before sleeping and they were all smeared with the dirt and soot that he could still feel caking his skin. Two-Tall Tim, his number two man and as tall as two of Akbar, kinda, wasn't in his bunk. His towel was missing from the hook.

Shower. Shower would be good. He grabbed his own towel and headed down the dark, narrow hall to the far end of the bunk house. Every one of the dozen doors of his smoke teams were still closed, smokies still sacked out. A glance down another corridor and he could see that at least a couple of the Mount Hood Aviation helicopter crews were up, but most still had closed doors with no hint of light from open curtains sliding under them. All of MHA had gone above and beyond on this one.

"Hey, Tim." Sure enough, the tall Eurasian was in one of the shower stalls, propped up against the back wall letting the hot water stream over him.

"Akbar the Great lives," Two-Tall sounded half asleep.

"Mostly. Doghouse?" Akbar stripped down and hit the next stall. The old plywood dividers were flimsy with age and gray with too many showers. The Mount Hood Aviation firefighters' Hoodie One base camp had been a kids' summer camp for decades. Long since defunct, MHA had taken it over and converted the playfields into landing areas for their helicopters, and regraded the main road into a decent airstrip for the spotter and jump planes.

"Doghouse? Hell, yeah. I'm like ten thousand calories short." Two-Tall found some energy in his voice at the idea of a trip into town.

The Doghouse Inn was in the nearest town. Hood River lay about a half hour down the mountain and had exactly what they needed: smokejumper-sized portions and a very high ratio of awesomely fit young women come to windsurf the Columbia Gorge. The Gorge, which formed the Washington and Oregon border, provided a fantastically target-rich environment for a smokejumper too long in the woods.

"You're too tall to be short of anything," Akbar knew he was being a little slow to reply, but he'd only been awake for minutes.

"You're like a hundred thousand calories short of being even a halfway decent size," Tim was obviously recovering faster than he was.

"Just because my parents loved me instead of tying me to a rack every night ain't my problem, buddy."

He scrubbed and soaped and scrubbed some more until he felt mostly clean.

"I'm telling you, Two-Tall. Whoever invented the hot shower, that's the dude we should give the Nobel prize to."

"You say that every time."

"You arguing?"

He heard Tim give a satisfied groan as some muscle finally let go under the steamy hot water. "Not for a second."

Akbar stepped out and walked over to the line of sinks, smearing a hand back and forth to wipe the condensation from the sheet of stainless steel screwed to the wall. His hazy reflection still sported several smears of char.

"You so purdy, Akbar."

"Purdier than you, Two-Tall." He headed back into the shower to get the last of it.

"So not. You're jealous."

Akbar wasn't the least bit jealous. Yes, despite his lean height, Tim was handsome enough to sweep up any ladies he wanted.

But on his own, Akbar did pretty damn well himself. What he didn't have in height, he made up for with a proper smokejumper's muscled build. Mixed with his tan-dark Indian complexion, he did fine.

The real fun, of course, was when the two of them went cruising together. The women never knew what to make of the two of them side by side. The contrast kept them off balance enough to open even more doors.

He smiled as he toweled down. It also didn't hurt that their opening answer to "what do you do" was "I jump out of planes to fight forest fires."

Worked every damn time. God he loved this job.

THE SMALL TOWN of Hood River, a winding half-an-hour down the mountain from the MHA base camp, was hopping. Mid-June, colleges letting out. Students and the younger set of professors high-tailing it to the Gorge. They packed the bars and breweries and sidewalk cafes. Suddenly every other car on the street had a windsurfing board tied on the roof.

The snooty rich folks were up at the historic Timberline Lodge on Mount Hood itself, not far in the other direction from MHA. Down here it was a younger, thrill seeker set and you could feel the energy.

There were other restaurants in town that might have better pickings, but the Doghouse Inn was MHA tradition and it was a good luck charm no smokie in his right mind messed with that. This was the bar where all of the MHA crew hung out. It didn't look like much from the outside, just a worn old brick building beaten by the Gorge's violent weather. Aged before its time, which had been long ago.

But inside was awesome. A long wooden bar stretched down one side with a half-jillion microbrew taps and a small but well-stocked kitchen at the far end. The dark wood paneling, even on the ceiling, was barely visible beneath thousands of pictures of doghouses sent from patrons all over the world. Miniature dachshunds in ornately decorated shoeboxes, massive Newfoundlands in backyard mansions that could easily house hundreds of their smaller kin, and everything in between. A gigantic Snoopy atop his doghouse in full Red Baron fighting gear dominated the far wall. Rumor said Shulz himself had been here two owners before and drawn it.

Tables were grouped close together, some for standing and drinking, others for sitting and eating.

"Amy, sweetheart!" Two-Tall called out as they entered the bar. The perky redhead came out from behind the bar to receive a hug from Tim. Akbar got one in turn, so he wasn't complaining. Cute as could be and about his height; her hugs were better than taking most women to bed. Of course, Gerald the cook and the bar's co-owner was big enough and strong enough to squish either Tim or Akbar if they got even a tiny step out of line with his wife. Gerald was one amazingly lucky man.

Akbar grabbed a Walking Man stout and turned to assess the crowd. A couple of the air jocks were in. Carly and Steve were at a little table for two in the corner, obviously not interested in anyone's company but each others. Damn, that had happened fast. New guy on the base swept up one of the most beautiful women on the planet. One of these days he'd have to ask Steve how he'd done that. Or maybe not. It looked like they were settling in for the long haul; the big "M" was so not his own first choice.

Carly was also one of the best FBANs in the business. Akbar was a good Fire Behavior Analyst, had to be or he wouldn't have made it to first stick—lead smokie of the whole MHA crew. But Carly was something else again. He'd always found the Flame Witch, as she was often called, daunting and a bit scary besides; she knew the fire better than it did itself. Steve had latched on to one seriously driven lady. More power to him.

The selection of female tourists was especially good today, but no other smokies in yet. They'd be in soon enough…most of them had groaned awake and said they were coming as he and Two-Tall kicked their hallway doors, but not until they'd been on their way out —he and Tim had first pick. Actually some of the smokies were coming, others had told them quite succinctly where they could go—but hey, jumping into fiery hell is what they did for a living anyway, so no big change there.

A couple of the chopper pilots had nailed down a big table right in the middle of the bustling seating area: Jeannie, Mickey, and Vern. Good "field of fire" in the immediate area.

He and Tim headed over, but Akbar managed to snag the chair closest to the really hot lady with down-her-back curling dark-auburn hair at the next table over —set just right to see her profile easily. Hard shot, sitting there with her parents, but damn she was amazing. And if that was her mom, it said the woman would be good looking for a long time to come.

Two-Tall grimaced at him and Akbar offered him a comfortable "beat out your ass" grin. But this one didn't feel like that. Maybe it was the whole parental thing. He sat back and kept his mouth shut.

He made sure that Two-Tall could see his interest. That made Tim honor bound to try and cut Akbar out of the running.

LAURA JENSON HAD SPOTTED them coming into the restaurant. Her dad was only moments behind.

"Those two are walking like they just climbed off their first-ever horseback ride."

She had to laugh, they did. So stiff and awkward they barely managed to move upright. They didn't look like first-time windsurfers, aching from the unexpected workout. They'd also walked in like they thought they were two gifts to god, which was even funnier. She turned away to avoid laughing in their faces. Guys who thought like that rarely appreciated getting a reality check.

Available at fine retailers everywhere.

ABOUT THE AUTHOR

M.L. Buchman started the first of over 60 novels, 100 short stories, and a fast-growing pile of audiobooks while flying from South Korea to ride his bicycle across the Australian Outback. Part of a solo around the world trip that ultimately launched his writing career in: thrillers, military romantic suspense, contemporary romance, and SF/F.

Recently named in *The 20 Best Romantic Suspense Novels: Modern Masterpieces* by ALA's Booklist, they have also selected his works three times as "Top-10 Romance Novel of the Year." His thrillers have been praised noting, "Tom Clancy fans will clamor for more."

As a 30-year project manager with a geophysics degree who has: designed and built houses, flown and jumped out of planes, and solo-sailed a 50' ketch, he is awed by what's possible. More at: www.mlbuchman.com.

Other works by M. L. Buchman: *(* - also in audio)*

Thrillers

Dead Chef
Swap Out!
One Chef!
Two Chef!

Miranda Chase
*Drone**
*Thunderbolt**
*Condor**

Romantic Suspense

Delta Force
*Target Engaged**
*Heart Strike**
*Wild Justice**
*Midnight Trust**

Firehawks
MAIN FLIGHT
Pure Heat
Full Blaze
*Hot Point**
*Flash of Fire**
Wild Fire
SMOKEJUMPERS
*Wildfire at Dawn**
*Wildfire at Larch Creek**
*Wildfire on the Skagit**

The Night Stalkers
MAIN FLIGHT
The Night Is Mine
I Own the Dawn
Wait Until Dark
Take Over at Midnight
Light Up the Night
Bring On the Dusk
By Break of Day

AND THE NAVY
Christmas at Steel Beach
Christmas at Peleliu Cove
WHITE HOUSE HOLIDAY
*Daniel's Christmas**
*Frank's Independence Day**
*Peter's Christmas**
*Zachary's Christmas**
*Roy's Independence Day**
*Damien's Christmas**
5E
Target of the Heart
Target Lock on Love
Target of Mine
Target of One's Own

Shadow Force: Psi
*At the Slightest Sound**
*At the Quietest Word**

White House Protection Force
*Off the Leash**
*On Your Mark**
*In the Weeds**

Contemporary Romance

Eagle Cove
Return to Eagle Cove
Recipe for Eagle Cove
Longing for Eagle Cove
Keepsake for Eagle Cove

Henderson's Ranch
*Nathan's Big Sky**
*Big Sky, Loyal Heart**
*Big Sky Dog Whisperer**

Love Abroad
Heart of the Cotswolds: England
Path of Love: Cinque Terre, Italy

Other works by M. L. Buchman:

Contemporary Romance (cont)

Where Dreams
Where Dreams are Born
Where Dreams Reside
Where Dreams Are of Christmas
Where Dreams Unfold
Where Dreams Are Written

Science Fiction / Fantasy

Deities Anonymous
Cookbook from Hell: Reheated
Saviors 101

Single Titles
The Nara Reaction
Monk's Maze
the Me and Elsie Chronicles

Non-Fiction

Strategies for Success
Managing Your Inner Artist/Writer
*Estate Planning for Authors**
Character Voice
*Narrate and Record Your Own Audiobook**

Short Story Series by M. L. Buchman:

Romantic Suspense

Delta Force
Delta Force

Firehawks
The Firehawks Lookouts
The Firehawks Hotshots
The Firebirds

The Night Stalkers
The Night Stalkers
The Night Stalkers 5E
The Night Stalkers CSAR
The Night Stalkers Wedding Stories

US Coast Guard
US Coast Guard

White House Protection Force
White House Protection Force

Contemporary Romance

Eagle Cove
Eagle Cove

Henderson's Ranch
*Henderson's Ranch**

Where Dreams
Where Dreams

Thrillers

Dead Chef
Dead Chef

Science Fiction / Fantasy

Deities Anonymous
Deities Anonymous

Other
The Future Night Stalkers
Single Titles